DUETS AND DOMINANCE

Pleasure Island Series

ANYA SUMMERS

Published by Blushing Books
An Imprint of
ABCD Graphics and Design, Inc.
A Virginia Corporation
977 Seminole Trail #233
Charlottesville, VA 22901

Anya Summers
Duets and Dominance

EBook ISBN: 978-1-947132-03-0
Print ISBN: 978-1-947132-35-1

Cover Art by ABCD Graphics & Design
v2

Cover Art by ABCD Graphics & Design

Chapter 1

Bad days were like last night's take out, easily disposable. You went to bed and the next morning, they were a thing of the past.

Bad lives were another matter.

The ferry sliced through rough seas so startlingly aquamarine as to seem like a foreign planet with the depths of its vibrant hue. The wind diminished the oppressive glare of the noonday sun in the near cloudless sky. In the distance, still a dark blip on the horizon, they cruised toward Pleasure Island, and what Lizzie hoped would be a week that would resuscitate her existence. She wanted a do over. Another chance to kick start her flailing life into a direction she wanted.

Lizzie didn't want pity. That was an emotion reserved for fools and drama queens. While she might have been naïve in her beliefs, she rarely allowed her emotions to get the better of her.

In some ways, her life had been blessed beyond measure. What did a little rich girl with every financial advantage know of misery? When it came to the material world, she'd never suffered, and knew just how lucky she was because of it. However, in other aspects—the ones that mattered most, and couldn't be bought, sold, or traded—her existence had been a series of disappointments and shortcomings, one after another.

Lizzie understood without a doubt what her parents, peers, and colleagues would think if she made her displeasure known. Her parents, Jonathan and Mary von Klepper, would direct her to seek psychiatric help and would then go on as if nothing untoward had occurred—merely writing her off for choosing to exist outside what they deemed acceptable behavioral parameters. They did not suffer fools or any softer emotions lightly. There were days when Lizzie wondered if her parents even loved each other, considering the lack of warmth and feeling in the von Klepper household. Now, if there was talk of mergers and acquisitions, that was another animal entirely.

Lizzie's peers and colleagues, among whom competition and status were prized above all else, would smirk blatantly to her face. They would be overjoyed, because they'd think she had finally succumbed to the pressures of touring and performing nonstop, of being so transient that there was no place she could call home, and while she might stand on a stage playing for thousands and receive adulation by the bucket load, her life continued to be an empty shell of an existence. And she knew without a doubt how they would react, should she give voice to the pain inside, because of the snickers and whispers that had been present over the last six months whenever she walked into rehearsal. Finding your fiancé in bed with another woman could do that to a girl. Finding the nefarious couple in your apartment and your bed, well, that was another level of hell entirely.

Seven years of her life, down the toilet. Seven years of waiting for Edward to marry her. Seven years of patiently waiting for him to make an honest woman out of her. God, how he and the model he'd been banging must have laughed over her stupidity.

It was absurd, really, how gullible she'd been in their relationship. Most men didn't want to wait to have a physical relationship, especially not with their intended bride.

Pretty stupid of her, in retrospect.

Lizzie rolled her eyes at herself and her predicament. Deep down, she had known that indisputable fact but she'd ignored the truth because she hadn't loved Edward. Hell, she hadn't been certain she even liked him. And he had obviously never cared for her, but had been as stuck as she in a prison of expectation.

She'd toed the line her parents had expected her to walk without overstepping the boundaries they erected. Because of that, she had lived a relatively sheltered life in pursuit of her career as a concert flutist. Even during her time at Julliard, she had been buttoned up with responsibilities and the terrible desire to please her parents, hoping that if she did as they asked of her, they would finally show a measure of warmth towards her.

So when her parents had introduced her to Edward Cunningham III, one of their friend's sons, it had been the most natural extension in the world to accept his proposal.

Sheltered, secluded, and undeniably obtuse when it came to matters of the heart, Lizzie had caved to their unspoken demands. It was funny now, for when she looked back at how Edward had proposed, it had obviously been another business merger and nothing more. There'd been no softer feelings or emotions involved. And if she felt there was something lacking between her and Edward, she believed it was her fault. That it was somehow her fault that she didn't generate great love from the people in her life. Even when she had such love to give, she couldn't seem to produce those feelings in those closest to her.

Granted, she wasn't totally defective in the love department. Lizzie knew she had a heart because of her love affair with music. Playing her flute was her safe space, which she poured her yearning heart into without repercussions or recriminations.

But it was no longer enough for Lizzie.

She wanted more from life. And she was determined to stop

feeling guilty over that fact. What she yearned for, what she craved, what woke her up at night with silent tears and a sob lodged in her throat because the dream had ended too soon, was passion. Break the bed, overturned furniture, can't get enough, heart-stopping passion.

No more safety nets for Lizzie. She'd lived her life in an insulated glass bubble: one she had every intention of shattering until it no longer existed.

Oh, she wanted romance and hearts and flowers too. Those were important and something on her internal list of things she wanted to achieve. But she also ached to be touched—and in a manner that wasn't infused with benign disinterest. Until recently, she had begun to wonder if passion outside of music was in the cards for her at all. She'd never experienced anything but lukewarm sensations with Edward. Maybe that was why it had been so easy to go along with no physical intimacy and the plan to wait until their wedding night before engaging in anything more than a few, rather tepid, awkward kisses.

Perhaps she would have continued toeing the line her parents and fiancé had set for her if the kiss with her best friend, Solomon, hadn't happened. Solomon had kissed Lizzie, and her brain had simply clicked off and a hunger, a burgeoning desire she'd not known existed, had overwhelmed her senses. With a single kiss, Solomon hadn't just knocked her socks off but hurled them into the farthest reaches of the galaxy.

But it *had* happened and she wasn't sorry in the slightest, even though she'd still been engaged to Edward. That stolen kiss at the McDougal wedding had left her aching and yearning for more. She'd desired more than a mere kiss that night, truth be told.

Lizzie had been the one to initiate their exchange in the conservatory after everyone had left for the reception hall. She'd slipped on the floor while stepping off the stage, and Solomon had caught her. Surrounded by his steely arms, pressed against the hard planes of his killer body, it had been the most natural thing to place her lips over his.

What she hadn't expected was for something so innocuous to alter the fabric of her life. As though, until she'd placed her lips over his, she'd been glimpsing the world askew and it had now suddenly been righted. The simple brush of her mouth over his had erupted into a wild fire.

Lizzie could still recall his flavor: dark and smoky with a hint of indubitable danger. The way his large hands had felt cupping her butt as she'd plastered herself against him. Even now, the memory caused torrents of need to flare up in her belly.

Solomon had stopped their off-the-charts kiss. He'd wrenched himself away, this man who'd been her best friend for thirteen years, and glowered at her, with hunger mingled with regret swimming in his gaze.

But she didn't feel remorse over her actions that night. Lizzie had never felt so alive as she had in Solomon's arms. Even though she had been engaged to another man, it had made her examine her life. Even if she hadn't walked in on Edward and the model, she had been planning to end things with him because their relationship was a farce.

Waltzing in on him boinking another woman had just been the final death knell and given Lizzie an easy excuse. However, Lizzie had a secret shame, one nobody knew.

She was the oldest effin' virgin in the world. And no, nuns didn't count.

As sad as it was, it was true. Elizabeth Annalise von Klepper, world-renowned flutist who'd played Carnegie Hall, with the London Symphony Orchestra, and had just completed a special guest appearance with the Philadelphia Philharmonic, was a thirty-one-year-old virgin. Lately, she'd been considering adopting a cat or two but that was too clichéd even for Lizzie.

She had never intended to maintain that status for so long. It just sort of happened. During her upbringing, like so many other aspects of the rest of her life, her sex life—or lack thereof—had been one of those boundaries her parents had erected for her. In high school and college, dating had not been acceptable or tolerated by her mom and dad. They had promised to help her choose a suitable husband when the time came, then emotionally manipulated her into going in the direction *they* chose for her life.

And they all knew how well that had worked out for Lizzie. About as well as trying to cuddle with an anaconda.

This week on Pleasure Island, she was on a mission. Not from God—he had nothing to do with it, unless she happened to scream his name in the throes of an orgasm. No, her mission was to get rid of that infernal moniker once and for all, satisfy her out of control hormones, and live a fuller, more balanced life.

The offer to perform with Solomon over Thanksgiving week had arrived like a gift and Lizzie had accepted without hesitation. She and Sol hadn't seen each other since Scotland and their one mind-bending kiss. But they were constantly in touch via technology. He was her best friend, and even though they tended to be on opposite sides of the world, they still managed to maintain contact. Even via simple text messages.

Despite the fact that they had studiously avoided the topic of their kiss entirely, Lizzie didn't plan to let him off the hook. Nope. If her plan worked, he would be the one to relieve her of her virgin status.

As for the holiday and forgoing spending it with family, her parents were no longer speaking to her since she'd called off her engagement to Edward, so it wasn't like she had plans. Not to mention, she still had to figure out where she would spend Christmas next month. While her parents might be just dandy with Edward screwing some tall, leggy model whose image was splashed over magazine covers everywhere, Lizzie wasn't. Regardless that she didn't have deeper feelings for him, she had tried to make herself care about Edward by attempting to bed him for years. And each time, he'd stopped her, because he said he wanted their wedding night to be their first time together. More like: he was already banging another chick and didn't want to accidently holler her name in the throes of climax.

In her naïveté, she'd thought him sweet and romantic, with his mild-mannered kisses that barely mustered a glimmer of interest in her. That chapter of her life was done. Lizzie was ready to commandeer her own vessel and choose who she wanted, purely because they made her feel.

She disembarked *The Leg Spreader*, helmed by a big bruiser of a man, Derek, his mocha skin stretched over what seemed like acres of muscles. He reminded her of those large gym rats who spent oodles of time pumping iron. While his ship's name was exactly what Lizzie wanted to have happen on Pleasure Island, the boat captain didn't seem like the ideal candidate to relieve her of her cherry. The man was too huge, and would likely not only take her maidenhead but split her five-foot, petite body asunder. Although, if it came down to the finish line this week, he'd do in a pinch. Especially since his black gaze regarded her with interest.

One way or the other, when she left Pleasure Island, she would no longer be a virgin.

Perhaps she was being overly dramatic about her situation. Maybe it wasn't the huge, gargantuan problem it felt like. It might possibly be better if she just picked a guy up in the bar and got the sordid deed over with. Then she could wash her hands of the issue once and for all.

But, in her heart of hearts, she wanted her first time to mean something to the recipient. Which was damn near impossible to accomplish in this day and age of sexting, and pick up lines via dick pictures, where people changed partners like they changed shoes.

And part of her issue had always been that she wasn't forward or outgoing like other women. She wasn't loud or outspoken, she didn't get jiggy with it and dance on table tops.

What she did do was play the flute better than anyone in the world. That had to count for something—or at least, she thought it did. Except the men she interacted with tended to be intimidated by her status, her success.

Lizzie had worked her ass off to get where she was, and had sacrificed years of her life to honing her discipline. There had also been that farce of an engagement, which she had to admit had worked on a surface level because she'd been too busy minding her career while giving off the image of having it all. The great career, snagging one of the most eligible bachelors for a fiancé, wealth both from her parents and the fortune she'd made on her own… But none of that shit mattered when you'd never been cuddled with in bed, or even hugged all that much. Lizzie yearned for affection.

And that was her two-ton elephant in the room.

In the six months since her split with Edward, she'd gone on a multitude of first dates but no second ones. Once the guy discovered what she did for a living, they skedaddled faster than a cockroach running for cover when the light was switched on. So why didn't she date some of the men she knew in orchestras? She could have snorted at the mere thought. With the way gossip traveled in their little epicenter, word would spread faster than a grease fire.

Most of the men were officious jackanapes, and once her virginal status was revealed, yikes. She winced at the thought. The embarrassment of it—much like the horrid dream of finding yourself naked in front of your classmates—and the revelation would send every jealous hound sniffing at her skirt for more details as to why she'd been engaged for an eternity and was still a virgin.

This week, Lizzie would change that status. She wanted sex, and lots of it. If she had to do the submissive thing this week, after and in between her performance to achieve that goal, fine. It wasn't a problem.

Fear beat wings inside her chest as she descended the gangway plank. The only problem would be convincing the man she wanted to lose her virginal status with. That was her true conundrum.

"Elizabeth, lass, welcome. It's a pleasure to see you again." This from the hunk of burning love, the sexy Scottish gent, Jared McTavish—who, word had it, was now engaged—and who stood on the docks waiting for her. Lizzie was certain that female hearts worldwide had broken because of his newly taken status. The man was simply beautiful, with his ginger hair loose and wavy in the morning sunlight, brushing his wide, broad shoulders which were covered by a crisp, white linen dress shirt. His breathtaking smile, in a tanned face that carried a hint of just how naughty a man he could be. His gorgeous torso tapered to his lean, narrow hips, encased in gray pinstripe slacks. It was a bleeding shame he couldn't do the honors for her. He was an impressive slab of man beefcake.

Having said that, the man she'd chosen for the dubious honor, Solomon, was doubly impressive, with potent dark sensuality. The thought of him made her air stutter in her lungs and a low burn ignite in her belly. Solomon was her target; he just didn't know it yet.

She took Jared's outstretched hand. "Please, call me Lizzie. Thank you for inviting me, Jared. I'm really looking forward to this week."

"I'm delighted that you could make it, what with the holiday this week, lass. Are you certain your family won't be missing you?" he asked, escorting her, with a casual hand against her back, to a waiting golf cart.

"I'm positive they won't." Miss her? They'd barely tolerated her existence, and that was before she'd broken off her engagement with Edward. If she attempted to bridge that gap Lizzie was certain they would make her wear a scarlet letter over her breast and perform self-flagellation at their behest.

"Well, on Thursday, you must have dinner with my fiancée and me. My Naomi is cooking a Thanksgiving feast for our immediate friends, and you are most welcome to attend," Jared offered, helping her into her seat. He walked with a sure-footed grace, which was uncommon for such a large man, around to the driver's side.

Lizzie had only met Jared once before, briefly, at the McDougal wedding nearly a year previously, and he was about as nice a man as they came. He was also an alpha Dom to his very core. A rather potent combination. His congenial offer suffused her with unexpected warmth. There was no subterfuge at work, no guessing what his intentions might be. It was a world away from what she'd known.

Jared drove like a man used to the world bending to his will, yet still managed to maintain a calm, steady air. The path rose from the docks in a gradual ascension. A riot of greenery and flowers of every color bloomed along the path. The warm breeze carried a hint of salt water and orchids. Lizzie replied, "That would be lovely, thank you. It's so pretty here."

It was a castaway paradise. What better place to lose her virginity?

Jared nodded, a magnanimous smile hovering over his lips. "It is. And since we are booked up this week, I have you in one of our suites in the main hotel. I hope that will suffice."

"Of course. I'm just pleased that you remembered me and extended the invitation. Frankly, staying in the hotel will make it easier with the shows. And I'm used to living on the road so a suite isn't a hardship, I assure you," she replied as they parked in a space near the ivory dome of the hotel.

The hotel itself had a unique, *Jetsons* like quality to it, what with the way it sloped up in a rounded shape, with the balconies for the rooms carved into the dome so that no ledge or overlook jutted out but gave it a smooth, space age appearance.

"That cannot be easy, the constant travel," Jared said, escorting her into the elevator.

"It certainly has its moments." *Like, for instance, cutting a trip short to find your fiancé in bed with another woman.*

"I'll bet. Let me show you where you will be playing first. Your luggage is being delivered to your suite, so you have nothing to worry about there. In your welcome packet, I've asked them to include a pair of island cuffs, if you've a mind to attend the club in the evenings. If you're not submissive, then don't worry about those. I just wanted to offer them in case," Jared explained.

Was Lizzie submissive? Gosh, she had no idea. A part of her thought she might be, but how did one know when one hadn't experienced sex?

Since she had no answer for him, she said, "Thanks for that."

She could determine later whether she needed to wear them or not. When the doors slid open, they stepped off the elevator and into the hotel lobby. Lizzie had performed in some of the grandest music halls ever built but when it came to this hotel, grand didn't even begin to describe it. While the exterior might look futuristic, the interior boasted a sublime elegance. The reservation desk and concierges, with their sleek lines, were on her left. Beyond the reservation desk was the entrance to a restaurant, *Master's Pleasure*, and beside it, a gift shop that appeared to offer everything, from grocery staples to island apparel and items for the kinky side of life. On her right was a seating area with leather couches and chairs, tropical plants in a profusion of leafy greens and riot of colors, which accented and softened the inherently masculine furniture. In the corner of the seating area was a glossy black Yamaha baby grand piano.

It was the man sitting on the piano bench, his long fingers—which she knew from a lifetime spent in his company—fiddling with the ivory keys that caused all the blood in her body to churn. Solomon Ventura, one of the finest piano players in the world, and the only man who'd ever kissed her brainless. Darkly sensual good looks. Tall and well built, especially for someone who spent his life sitting at a piano bench.

Lizzie hadn't known what to expect when she saw him. They'd been friends, the best of friends, for more than a decade. Until the night of that fateful kiss. It had been nearly a year since then. Since she'd had her world turned inside out.

Solomon took her breath away. He always had, but she'd never understood the emotions she felt until the first touch of his lips on hers. His midnight hair was shorter than the last time they'd seen one another, and he had a smattering of dark stubble growth on his square jaw that was new. It made him seem more raw, less refined, and caused a low burn in her midsection. His skin always carried a trace of a tan, in contrast to her own ivory skin that wouldn't hold color to save her life. His broad shoulders moved with a sinuous grace, muscles rippling beneath his heather gray Henley, which sculpted and fit his chest: defining, and outlining how ripped his body was as his hands moved over the keyboard.

The man, quite simply put, made love to his instrument. It was the only way Lizzie could describe how Solomon played the keyboard. His entire body was fluid and intense, leaning and swaying as his fingers moved effortlessly. He caressed the black and white keys, stroking them to sounds as he wanted them to, and left the crowd panting, wanting more. It was exactly what Lizzie believed love should be, especially the first time. Maybe she was naïve, and that wasn't how the world really worked. But in her opinion, it was how it *should* work.

She felt the same way about the flute.

"Lizzie," Solomon said the moment he spied her, his deep, smooth baritone sliding over her like melted butter as a smile spread across his handsome face. It all had the effect of an atom bomb on her erogenous zones. He unfolded himself from the bench and stood. All six feet two inches of power packed muscle emerged from behind the piano.

"Sol. You're well, I take it?" She lifted her face as he enveloped her in a friendly embrace. His gunmetal gray eyes were full of delight and the warmth of friendship.

Lizzie returned his hug but felt awkward. The knowledge that she was planning to try and seduce one of her oldest friends caused tension to enter her frame.

"Very. I'm glad you decided to join me this week so we can do what we do best together," Solomon said, with an overly dramatic wiggle of his dark brows. She couldn't help the laugh that escaped, or the fact that the inherently sexy innuendo stirred her blood. She sighed internally when he released her. All she wanted was to sink into his embrace and stay there.

"Will this location work for you both?" Jared asked, glancing between them. Lizzie noted that, while she found Jared attractive, Sol eclipsed him. It didn't make Jared any less handsome. It was just that, for her, Solomon's energy overrode everything else. And his dark woodsy scent that surrounded her when he had hugged her, seemed to linger. It made her want to curl into him.

"Yes. The acoustics are fine and will work for our duets." Solomon slid his hands into the pockets of his Levi's. His jeans contoured the long lines of his powerful legs.

"But?" Jared gave Solomon a glance with a raised eyebrow.

Solomon shrugged, confident and at ease as he replied, "Well, it wasn't built as a music hall but it should work for our purposes here this week. Once you get the outdoor theater built, I'd love to try that out."

Jared assimilated that information, respect for Solomon in his gaze, and said, "Good enough. I'll keep you in mind for a return engagement once it's complete. You both have today to get yourselves settled. Then three shows a day starting Monday—tomorrow. I have the times marked in your registration packets that I had delivered to your rooms. They are next to one another, so you will be close—since you mentioned, Solomon, that you'd want to rehearse."

"What do you say, Lizzie, shall we go up and reacquaint ourselves with each other?" Solomon shot her a sideways grin.

She knew he meant it in a friendly manner. That was Sol. He was a charmer, always up for a good time, with a glimmer in his eyes and flash of teeth in his smile. But somehow along the way (and if she were honest with herself it was before the wedding kiss last year), she'd begun to yearn for him, imagine him in a way no friend should. Most people didn't look at their best friend and wonder what they looked like naked.

But she had. And on more than one occasion.

Solomon slipped her arm through his and said, "Come, mia bella, I've been waiting in agony to play with you once again."

At his suggestion, she clenched her free hand, digging her nails into her palm to keep herself from audibly sighing. There would be time this week to address the fact that his words turned her insides into an aching mass of need. Instead of launching herself into his arms, she acted like they always did, twining her arm more solidly through his and replied, "Lead the way, my friend."

Chapter 2

R elief flooded Solomon.

Lizzie was acting like nothing had occurred between them. She didn't mention Scotland and the kiss he couldn't seem to forget. Ever since, he'd lain awake at night, remembering how she'd felt against him, how she'd tasted. Solomon had jacked off to the memory of it more times than he cared to admit. Because, admittedly, it had only been a fucking kiss.

But she had rocked his world with it. The first taste of her, the tiny sounds she'd made in the back of her throat, the way she'd fit in his arms. It had taken herculean effort to prevent himself from slaking his thirst for her that night.

Solomon was glad she'd not brought it up. Ever since that night, he'd had to work overtime and pretend like it hadn't mattered, hadn't happened. It was good she had moved on from their kiss, even if he'd had difficulty. It was for the best that they both ignored what had happened in Scotland and continued on with their lives, as friends. Friends didn't go around kissing each other. Friends didn't go around jacking off to the thought of said kiss with that friend either.

This place would be good for him. He already planned to stay past their performance week. If he had to fuck his way through the sub pool on the island—as well as any single subs who visited—to thoroughly evict Lizzie from his lustful thoughts and put her back squarely in the friend column, then that was what he was going to do.

The private balcony off his room had a clear view of the ocean. The waves undulated, an endless movement of shimmering turquoise and cobalt. Sol inhaled a few steadying breaths. Lizzie wasn't for him. She was too pure, too sweet, and just too good for a man like him.

But Christ did she look good, better even than when he'd seen her in Scotland.

Lizzie was the type of woman suited to candlelight and gentle lovemaking. Sol wasn't that kind of man, never had been. It wasn't that he wasn't a good man, he just wasn't good for her. She wouldn't survive his brand of love, and Solomon couldn't be satisfied without being a Dominant.

That didn't mean he'd forget that one stolen kiss. Far from it. One touch, a simple brushing of lips, and every part of his being had stampeded to the forefront, eager to stake its claim. That Lizzie belonged to him.

If only that were true.

They were friends. It was better that way. She deserved better. Were he to turn the full brunt of his desires in her direction, she'd run screaming into the night. As she should, because a good girl shouldn't tangle with the big bad wolf. His brand of dominance would leave her shattered. Solomon must have control, otherwise it put him on a slippery slope toward utter ruin.

And he'd never be able to live with himself if he destroyed such perfection.

At the soft knock on his door, he said over his shoulder, "Come in."

And there she was, his *mia piccolo bella*, his little beauty. Lizzie was small, delicate, and fine-boned. She reminded him of the kind of pixie sprite that one would imagine serving Oberon in *A Midsummer Night's Dream*. A good foot shorter than he, her golden hair was pulled back at her nape. A few wisps had escaped the bun and made her appear downright delectable.

In her low-rise jeans, snug and form-fitting around the slight curve of her hips, and silk blouse that reminded him of the poppy fields in bloom in Tuscany, she looked like a little Miss Prim and Proper. God, did he want to muss her up, in more ways than one. Her face was exquisite, with strong cheekbones, and was delicate just like the rest of her. Age had made her face more striking, the softness of youth having faded and turning her into an incredibly gorgeous woman, with skin like a pearlescent dew drop and unmarred, with a pert nose and over generous smile tossed into the mix. Gazing at the top-heavy lip that was curved in a gamine grin as she regarded him, Solomon remembered sucking on it. But it was her eyes, big, luminescent jade green jewels that always seemed to pull him in.

"Where would you like to begin?" she asked, her voice melodious, as if it had absorbed some of the properties of her flute. If only she knew. He'd like to strip her bare. See how the globes of her sexy ass would look with cane marks marring her flesh. Discover what she looked like as she came around his cock... in her mouth, in her pussy, and even her pretty rosette he was damn sure no one had taken yet. Not his Lizzie, and certainly not by that ex-prick of her fiancé. He could imagine leaving his mark on her breasts, her belly, and the tender flesh of her inner thighs. He sucked in a ragged breath, attempting to cool his ardor and douse the incessant lust.

Not for me.

He sat at his portable Yamaha keyboard and bench, which traveled with him everywhere. He tended to be hell on airlines because of it. But he never liked being far from his instrument and the fact was, it was rather difficult to cart a grand piano.

He covered the desire hammering through him and hoped she had not noticed the erection he'd been sporting. For appearances' sake, until he could somehow remove her from his dreams, he was strictly business. And if he was dying to feel her in his arms again, hear her throaty moans as he laid siege to her composure, no one would be the wiser—least of all Lizzie.

"I'd thought we'd begin with Mozart's *Concerto number eleven*," he said, withdrawing the music from a large binder he'd set on the nearby end table.

"That old thing. We're here to entertain the guests, not put them into a coma," Lizzie said with an eye roll, her hands going to her hips. Only Lizzie was confident enough to challenge him.

"What's wrong with Mozart? You always seem to diss his music," Solomon jibed. This was what they were good at: friendly banter that, at times, had been known to escalate into shouting matches. But they always came back together and apologized. It was their way, had been since they'd first met at Julliard a million years ago.

"Nothing's wrong with him per se but his music is a bit dull. What about Franz Schubert's *Ständchen*?" she replied.

"Now we are really hitting the snooze button on the shows," he kidded her, and a blush spread across her cheeks. He'd have paid to be able to read her thoughts.

Lizzie fidgeted, her thumb and forefinger pinching her lip as she looked at the music stand and the selection he'd already arranged. He'd love to replace her thumb with his, see if her pink tongue would dart out to taste him. He ground his teeth as she said, "Well, what if we included some holiday music? I realize it's only Thanksgiving—"

"In America."

"Er, right, but with Christmas only a few short weeks away, it wouldn't be all that bad. Plus, this is a different crowd than we normally play to. I don't want to get laughed out of here, do you?" she asked him, looking for all the world like an enchantress bent on stealing his sense of honor.

"Mia bella, no one will laugh at you while you play. It's an impossibility," he assured her. How she wasn't aware of her own appeal baffled him. To Solomon, her beauty sucker-punched him every time. When she played her instrument, she transformed into this stunning creature and drew people to her. Himself included. Lizzie played with the very fabric of her soul on display, and it awed him every fucking time. From the first time he'd witnessed her performance when they were at Julliard, and every show they'd performed together since then. She enchanted when she performed, a golden goddess among mere mortals who wished to worship her.

It was why he'd been unable to stop himself from kissing her at the McDougal wedding. She'd shone brighter than even the bride as she'd played that night, and when she'd fallen into his arms and tentatively brushed her lips against his, he'd been lost. He'd mortgage his very soul for another taste. But he'd condemn them both to hell if he did.

"I very much doubt that. Believe me. It's happened quite a bit over the last six months," Lizzie said, shifting her gaze, but not before he caught the pain held within. He couldn't trust himself to touch her and not want her, as much as he wanted to pull her into his arms and comfort her. Solomon knew about that bonehead ex-fiancé of hers. How that idiot could choose a lifeless doll of a woman over Lizzie was beyond him. He'd give up everything for a night in her arms.

Instead of doing what his Dom soul urged him to do, which was scoop her up, console her, comfort her, and let her bathe him with her tears, he played it off, giving her a fierce look and saying, "Who do I need to beat up for you? Hmm? Who's been saying nasty things about you?"

With a gentle smile, she shook her head and murmured, "I

couldn't let you wreck your hands that way. Anyhow, it's just the fallout from my breakup with Edward. You know the gossip mill in our world. I appreciate that you want to play white knight for me."

"That I do. Not to worry, soon those old biddies will have someone else to mercilessly terrorize. And if not, just tell me who they are and I will deal with them," Solomon promised. But he wasn't a white knight by any means and would make some inquiries. No one harmed his Lizzie and got away with it. Not on his watch. And while it might be the only way he could protect her, he would do so until his dying breath.

"Hard to ignore it when what they say is true; I was a blind idiot. But enough about my broken engagement, I really don't want to rehash it any longer. It's done." She was trying to appear tough but he knew her inside and out.

"Lizzie, mia bella," he murmured, sympathy clouding his voice. Her pain sliced him to the bone. Solomon wished he could fix it for her, make it all go away, protect her from the vipers to be found in every corner of their world.

"It's fine, Sol. If you want us to start with Mozart, we can. But you know I'm a Brahms and Beethoven girl. As long as we can mix in some of their pieces, along with a few holiday songs, I think the crowd will enjoy it," she said, seeming to want to please him while changing the subject.

He regarded her. The fact that she hid her heartbreak and changed the subject on him, redirecting it toward work, told him more than anything that she was still hurting. Deep down, he knew it was for the best that they keep it friendly, contained, so that he wasn't tempted to console her—with his mouth. Perhaps when he no longer wanted her to distraction, then he could be the friend she needed to lean on and gather her close. He'd just have to find a willing sub tonight, once they were finished. Perhaps if he was balls-deep in another female, he could get the one he could never have out of his mind.

"See, I knew you'd see it my way," he ribbed her, attempting to change the mood to a more jovial, light-hearted one.

"Uh huh, just don't be surprised when people start nodding off to Mozart's *Concerto*," Lizzie warned with a gamine grin that didn't quite reach her eyes.

Shrugging off the need that constantly barraged his system whenever Lizzie was near, he shifted gears and moved his hands over the keys. Lizzie settled her flute at her too sexy mouth, her eyes trained on him. Her foot tapped the beat.

And then they began. The ivory keys were merely an extension of his hands as he played. All the tension, the need, morphed and flowed into his fingers, feeding the melody. It was a harmonic dance between them. Had been since their very first duet. There were very few musicians on the planet Solomon thought highly of. They were all needy bastards and could be rather obtuse and egotistical when it came down to it. But his Lizzie—dammit, she wasn't his. Except, perhaps, she was, and this was the one arena in which he was able to seduce her.

She seduced him every time. He only had to take a look at her. She glowed. Her soul and her heart were on display even as she performed a song she considered a one-way ticket to narcolepsy. Her eyes slid shut on the final note, as if to extend the pleasure of the pitch-perfect resonance.

He hid the fact that he was hard, that he wanted to strip her out of her prim and proper clothing and discover whether she did the same thing when she climaxed. He ordered, "Again."

Lizzie opened her eyes and glared. "It's a good thing I kinda like you, otherwise I'd be using my flute as a club right about now."

"You'd never physically hurt me, mia bella," he chided.

"Wanna bet?" She gave him a forthright glare that challenged every inch of his dominant nature. If she were his, he would turn her over his knee for that remark. Or better yet, make sure her mouth was too busy to speak at all.

He gritted his teeth at the unbidden sexual flare, and growled, "Are you attempting to irk me or do you just get off on being a pain in my ass?"

She cocked her head to the side, shifted her body, and said, "Well, it is Sunday and you know very well I have it marked on my calendar. Be sure to annoy Solomon today. I have a reminder set in my phone and everything."

He chuckled darkly. "I've missed having you around, Lizzie. Don't ever change for anyone. Now, if you will, again."

"If I must, I must." She sighed like he was forcing her to eat Brussels sprouts, which he knew she had a loathing for.

They played through each piece, selecting and discarding some, improvising on a few, until they felt they not only had a grasp on the material but were playing it perfectly without fail. Sol found that Lizzie was pure joy to perform with, even as they argued over the correct inflection in a stanza or sniped at one another for missing a beat.

"Well, mia bella, I think we can say we are as prepared as possible for our concerts this week. What do you say we call it a night?" he suggested. Because he needed to escape her presence before he did something that he would never be able to take back.

"Yes, I believe so. Was it good for you?" she teased.

A ball of lust slammed into him like a sledgehammer to the solar plexus. Christ, what he wouldn't give to have her beneath him, uttering those words. Both of them too spent and too satiated to move. With his bed so nearby, it wasn't a hard leap at all to imagine. He cleared his throat and said, "It always is with you. Now, I'm not sure about you, but I'm famished."

"Why don't we order room service?" Lizzie offered over her shoulder as she put her flute away. She was bent over at the waist. The taut globes of her jeans-covered ass pointed at him invitingly.

"I was hoping to avail myself of the restaurant and club now that we're done for the day. You're welcome to join me in the restaurant for dinner if you like." Solomon wanted to smack himself for the offer, but he was helpless and rather hopeless when it came to Lizzie. As much as he tended to suffer, he couldn't ever leave her, nor let her believe for one second he wasn't first and foremost her friend. He knew how cold her parents and her upbringing had been. Fuck, he'd met the vaulted von Kleppers, and had no idea how Lizzie had not only survived those cold fish, but ended up being the warm, generous, spunky woman she was around him.

"I'm not sure I'm fit for other company right now. If you could stop by my room on your way down, I have something for you," she said, her cheeks flushed, and she glanced away quickly so he couldn't read her eyes. What the devil was Lizzie up to? Sol had to admit he was curious, and since he was already feeling guilty for not taking her up on her offer to spend the evening with her, as friends, he caved.

"All right, give me fifteen minutes and I'll be over," he responded. That would give him time to change and prepare for dinner and the club. Not to mention get rid of the hard on he'd been sporting with her so very close by.

She blushed an even deeper shade of near mauve and said, "Okay, I will see you then."

Bemused, he watched her leave his room. And if he stared at the taut, lithe lines of her back or her perfectly rounded derrière a little too intensely, well, he was likely going to hell anyhow. Besides, he was the one who was tortured day in and out over what he would never have.

Chapter 3

This was it, the moment she'd been waiting for with Solomon.

She could do this: be brave. He'd not mentioned their kiss, but oh how she wished he would have, as it would make what she was about to do so much easier.

Lizzie entered her room. It was identical to Solomon's, only a mirror image. The suite was gorgeous, with plush furniture meant to entice a person. Kick back, relax, and have some wild and crazy sex if you've a mind to, considering how well stocked the armoire was with all manner of erotic toys. Then there was the fact that, in addition to the small kitchen and seating area, beyond the giant oak four-poster bed, was a padded horse.

Would Solomon want to put her on the thing? Restrain her? She knew he was a Dominant, even if she wasn't certain about all that entailed. To be with him, she would learn. She had already looked online, researching, and what she'd found had made her blush fire engine red. To her surprise, it had also sent her sadly neglected hormones into overdrive and aroused her.

Lizzie's heart was beating like a galloping horse down the final lap of a race. It was time. Tonight was the night. Her grand master plan to lose her virginity once and for all was about to be put into motion. In a battle against the clock, she changed out of her jeans and blouse, stripped off her panties and bra, and slid on a silk robe the color of sunset. Removing the pins holding her hair back, she let it fall loose. After being in a bun all day, her normally straight hair held soft waves, and curled enticingly over her back and shoulders.

She brushed her teeth, because, for her first time, she didn't want to have dragon breath. Then she nearly dropped her toothbrush at the solid knock on her door. Forget butterflies, Lizzie had jackrabbits hopping in her belly.

"Come in," she called out from the bathroom. Her voice sounded breathy and uncertain, even to her ears. The click of her suite door opening and closing nearly sent her into a panic attack and abort mission sequence.

Stop being a ninny! You've wanted Sol forever. Just do it!

"Lizzie, what's going on, mia bella, are you all right?" Solomon asked, his smooth baritone sliding through her core like warm molasses. With a last glance in the mirror, she inhaled a steadying breath and exited the bathroom. Her knees weak, she kept her spine straight and her head high.

Solomon's gaze snapped instantly from congenial to a dark and forbidding scowl. He scorched her with a look, his gaze traveling from her head down to her toes and back up. Her breath clogged in her throat. Her nipples beaded into hard points as fear and desire intertwined.

Solomon murmured, his voice gruff, "Lizzie, mind telling me what this is about? I thought you said you had something for me."

"I do," she responded. Then she unbelted the silk tie at her waist and slid the robe off her shoulders. It flowed like water into a puddle at her feet. She kept her gaze on his despite the shocked expression on his face. Clenching her hands to stop the trembling, she said, "It's me. I want you, Sol. I want to be with you tonight. Instead of you going to the club and finding a woman, a submissive, to spend the evening with, I want you to take me to your bed."

Lizzie knew that what she was doing, dropping her clothes like this and throwing herself at him, was a huge risk. The last thing she wanted to do was drive a wedge between them or lose her best friend. But after that one kiss, she knew he was the only man she wanted, the only one she trusted. The air thickened with the potent energy that always seemed to dominate when they were near one another.

Her heart thudded against her chest. Her stomach clenched as she waited in agony for him to respond. It felt like hours passed as he stood erect, staring at her. Solomon was quite simply heart-rending, and so damn sexy. His gaze was unfathomable, his eyes blazed, turning them molten. His hands were clasped at his sides.

He was beautiful and erotic in his leather club gear. His pants rode low over his lean hips and seemed molded to his powerful thighs. Lizzie's gaze shuddered to a halt at his crotch. The man was hard, erect, and straining against the confines of his pants. Oh god, he was huge—everywhere. She had the insane worry crop up that he wouldn't fit her. But surely, once he was out of his pants and laid bare, he wouldn't be that big. Surely not.

She'd never seen him in black leather before. It made him seem dangerous, and erotic, and she wished he would turn around so she could see what his ass looked like. She knew it would be amazing, but she couldn't help that thought as she waited. Liquid pulls of heat cascaded through her as she caressed his ripped shoulders with her gaze. Her mouth was dry and yet she wanted to know how he tasted. Run her tongue along the hollow of his throat. Her nipples were hard points and her breasts seemed to swell beneath his hypnotic glare.

If Lizzie weren't so nervous, she'd mention how sexy he looked tonight, that he was all she could think about, and would he please strip now, too, so she could see all of him. She'd tell him how he made her knees weak with his carnal beauty. An ache thrummed in her chest, expanding as she waited for him to move, to say something, anything.

She would have laughed at the frozen tableau if there wasn't a sinking sensation of dread growing in the pit of her stomach as the seconds ticked by and still Solomon stood erect and unmoving.

"Sol, say something. Please," she murmured, unsure of what to do since she'd never been in this situation before. She had read in *Cosmo* that if you wanted to get a guy and were nervous, you should drop your clothes and see what happens. That most guys couldn't resist a naked woman and that it was a surefire way to get them into bed. Moisture seeped into the corners of her eyes.

Solomon finally moved, his steps filled with purpose. His long legs ate up the distance between them. A smile began to form on her lips as he neared. Her heart took flight.

And then everything went wrong.

Instead of reaching for her, he bent down, snatched her robe from its spot in a heap on the floor, and rose. Then he wrapped the robe around her shoulders, covering her frame.

"Get dressed, Lizzie. I don't know what game you think you're playing at, but I'll not be playing it. Not tonight, not ever. I'm going to walk out that door and pretend this never happened," Solomon bit out. His anger lashed against her and she flinched like she'd been struck.

She clutched the robe as he turned his back on her and strode toward the door. His muscles bunched and flowed as he moved with lion-like grace.

"Why? Why will you sleep with anything else with tits, but I'm this pariah? I know you felt something when you kissed me in Scotland. Why are you doing this? Am I that hideous to you?" Lizzie stared at his back, imploring him with her eyes to change course, erase the last few seconds. She was so ready for this change, and she had been certain he had felt it too.

With her words hanging in the air, Solomon stopped at the door. His hand gripped the handle but he didn't glance back at her. It was like he was ashamed of her. His voice, when he spoke, was low and devoid of emotion. "I'm not the man for you, Lizzie. And I never will be."

Then he left the room. The door slid quietly shut behind him. Ten thousand arrows piercing her chest would have been a kinder fate. She slid bonelessly to the floor, staring at the door, a sob lodged in her chest.

What should she do now that the one person she'd always counted on had turned his back on her?

Chapter 4

S olomon did not stop his feet and marched directly to the club. It was either that or head back to Lizzie's room and give her what she'd asked for. Problem was, he'd fuck her all night long until they were too exhausted to move—and she'd end up broken. When the elevator doors slid open on the second floor, he saw that the Dungeon Club was completely empty; closed until later that evening.

Fuck! Shit!

He swore under his breath. What did a guy have to do around here to get a drink? He snarled in the back of his throat as he fought against every instinct to head back up to Lizzie's room and claim what she'd so readily offered. Solomon couldn't be it. Couldn't be the vanilla, upstanding sort of guy she needed.

He stomped back to the elevator and headed down to the lobby. Surely the gift shop sold alcohol. Inside the small store, he avoided the lifestyle section, ignoring the clamps and Velcro restraints even though in his mind he could see Lizzie strapped to his bed, writhing beneath his touch while he took her where no man ever had before. He nearly lost his resolve to stay away from her.

Her image was scalded into his memory banks.

The grocery side of the store held boxed meals to go, and precisely what he needed. Grabbing one of the to go meals and a bottle of Patron silver, he headed out of the hotel, his feet leading him automatically down to the beach. In no mood for company tonight, Solomon reclined on one of the lounge chairs, ate a loaded sub sandwich, and sipped tequila directly from the bottle. There was no way he could attend the club tonight. He would be too tempted to head back up those three floors and take what Lizzie had offered.

He swallowed another dram. The tequila seared a path into his belly.

He only prayed that by morning he could erase the image of his Lizzie, naked and trembling before him. Solomon had been stunned silent, unprepared for seeing her in all her bountiful glory. He'd fantasized about her so often, and yet she'd blown every fantasy he had right out of the water. She was drop dead gorgeous—as he knew she would be—with her pert, high breasts that would fit in his hands nicely. The rouge-tipped nipples, beaded, and inviting his ravenous mouth. Her waist was small enough that he was sure his hands could span it easily. And the curve of her hips, the delicate hip bones, and flat stomach. Down to the triangle of her sex, devoid of hair. He'd been struck dumb. His mouth had watered to taste her, spread her supple thighs, and feast on her most sensitive flesh.

It had taken every ounce of strength he possessed to leave her room. His blood had rushed in his ears and he'd wanted to fall on her, fuck her until her legs came off, and satiate the sadistic beast inside. Lizzie was fragile, meant to be loved sweetly, and would never survive his need to dominate every fiber of her being and mark her, claim her as his.

Because he would, if he allowed his control to slip for one instant around her. The destruction he'd wreak upon her didn't bear thinking about. And he would, make no mistake, for he was a selfish bastard.

He tossed back another draught of tequila, focusing on the way it scorched a trail into his stomach instead of the arousal he felt, or the fact that his dick was straining against his leather pants, eager to be buried in her welcoming heat. Need clawed at him, shaking the core of his foundation. He tipped the bottle back, letting the burn do its worst. Maybe then he could convince himself as to why he shouldn't just go claim her. Lizzie wanted him. Christ, what a mess.

He wanted to howl at the moon, at the unfairness of it all. His Lizzie craved him. Solomon should be thrilled, but he all he could muster was a deep sorrow. She'd clearly been as affected as he by their one kiss in Scotland. The one that should never have occurred, and yet had been imprinted on his psyche like a brand.

Perhaps if he'd been able to forget about her in the months since their kiss, things would have been different, but short of a lobotomy, nothing could make him erase it from his memory banks. The way she'd plastered herself to him. And just how sweet she'd tasted, like the finest Bordeaux. He'd never expected her mouth to be this carnal fantasy brought to life, but for him, it had been.

One simple decision on her part had smashed all his carefully laid plans to smithereens. He should be furious with her. She'd screwed them both without realizing it. The Dom in him wanted to take her across his knee for pulling a stunt like this. He'd fantasized about her plenty over the years, but nothing had lived up to the reality. Now, he'd never be free. The harder he tried to forget, the more insistent the imagery.

Dammit! Having planned to go to the club and lose himself in a pretty sub with no strings attached, Sol knew there was no point now: they'd be a pallid imitation and leave him wanting. So he kept himself away from the hotel, because he feared he would either imagine it was Lizzie, or the experience would be so lack-luster, he'd seek her out and that would push him over the edge.

Solomon reclined on the chaise, still sipping tequila. The Milky Way sparkled above him, illuminating the expanse of night sky. The quarter moon reflected off the ocean tide, turning it into an endless sea of silver as it rolled in and out.

Drinking a fifth of tequila, alone on the beach, wasn't how he had planned to spend his evening. Christ, why had she done it? Changed the nature of their relationship? Didn't she realize he was doing this with her best interests at heart? She deserved a vanilla guy like her ex-fiancé, who would never even contemplate the multitude of erotic and sinfully explicit fantasies Sol's brain could conjure up. She was delicate and refined, deserved soft candlelight and flowers, not whips and handcuffs.

As long as he lived, he didn't think he'd ever get the sight of her, bared to him, out of his mind. It was like it had been engraved on his soul. From the first moment he'd met her, when she'd been a freshman and he a junior at Julliard, he'd been struck by her poignant beauty. Her beguiling jade eyes had haunted his dreams since the very first.

Solomon had been leaving band practice when this tiny blonde whirlwind had barreled into him in his practice room on her way to class. She'd been lost, and worried she would miss her next class, fumbling, her small hands a flurry of butterfly wings against him as she checked to make sure she hadn't hurt him. He was twice her size and she'd been worried that she'd injured him.

Solomon had walked her to class then, the little pixie sprite slip of a woman he'd wanted to protect from the world. And the first order of business had been protecting her from himself. He'd spied the innocence and wonder in her gaze as she looked up at him, blushing furiously, and knew that, as much as he wanted her, he could never touch her. He had already been indoctrinated into the BDSM lifestyle and knew that he needed to dominate.

Lizzie was fragile, like a flower blooming in the spring which too much force would rip to shreds. So Sol had slipped a shield around his soul and adopted the moniker of best friend, telling himself that keeping her at arm's length while still keeping her in his life was for the best.

And he knew it had been the right decision, but Christ, he wasn't a fucking saint. Lizzie had no idea how close she'd come to being well and truly screwed.

By the time he'd finished the bottle, the Milky Way was blurring, reflected on the ocean. A shooting star rocketed across the pitch black sky but he didn't wish upon it, because even a wish was moot for the likes of him. Telling Lizzie no, turning her down, as much as it had killed him to do, had been the right course of action, the honorable way to handle it. A warm Caribbean breeze swept over him, carrying a hint of salt water. Solomon's eyes slid shut and he muttered a curse.

What a mess. One thing was for certain, his Lizzie was all woman. He'd always be there for her because she was his best friend—he just couldn't give her what she needed. He drifted off to sleep with the tide serenading him.

Chapter 5

Everything had blown up in her face.

She had no one to blame but herself. Perhaps she should have pushed the issue after the kiss last year. It had knocked her off her axis and she'd needed time to find her center of gravity again. She felt sick to her stomach.

Although that may also have been because she'd ordered room service after the debacle, needing bucket-loads of chocolate. Instead of a healthy dinner, she'd had a brownie sundae à la mode, with extra fudge sauce, and a bottle of rosé.

One thing was for certain, Lizzie had cried more last night than she had upon discovering Edward with the model in her bed; more than when her parents had cut her out of their lives because she'd broken the engagement and refused to renege; more than after the snickers she'd received during rehearsal at the orchestra when it all became public knowledge. There was something inherently wrong that people derived such pleasure from watching others fail, especially those who were further up the success ladder.

When he'd left her room last night, the hope she had that Solomon possibly wanted more with her had been lost. It had been the shining, glistening jewel she had clutched to her chest, which had seen her through the past six months. The hope that there was more between them than friendship. It had kept her going, even when everything else went wrong. Losing that hope, the intangible possibility, Lizzie felt like a bomb had gone off in her chest. There was now a big empty hole where her heart had once resided.

She prayed he wouldn't cut her out completely. She could live without a lot, but she couldn't live without Solomon in her life in some capacity. He was her best friend, and she couldn't lose him, not over her foolishness.

Lizzie glanced at her haggard appearance in the mirror. After a night of tears, she looked like the crypt keeper. Eyes, red-rimmed and puffy, dark circles from lack of sleep, her face drawn. It took an hour with her makeup skills to hide the signs of her distress. A few eye-drops cleared the red out, for the most part. But if someone looked closely enough, they'd see the strain.

However, for the purposes of performing today, it would work. No one would notice that she was walking around with her heart broken in two. That Solomon turning her down the way he had, had hurt worse than walking in on her ex and finding him screwing another woman.

His parting words would live with her forever. "I'm not the man for you, Lizzie. And I never will be." As though they had been inscribed upon her soul. What did that even mean: that he wasn't for her?

Stop it! Lizzie yelled at herself. She couldn't think about Solomon, or what he'd said last night. It was bad enough that she had to perform with him in fifteen minutes and pretend as though nothing was amiss. If she remembered last night, she'd slide into a sobbing mess. Which would toss a monkey wrench into her new plan to rid herself of her virginal state.

Overnight, in the wee hours, after far too much contemplation and self-condemnation, Lizzie had made a decision. Once she knew that her friendship with Solomon wasn't over, she had to move on. So Sol didn't want her that way. He was still her best friend, and she loved him. And she knew he loved her—just not in the way she'd hoped.

But that didn't mean *someone* on this infernal island wouldn't want her, and might, in the end, help her push past yearning for her best friend. She wasn't an ogre. Perhaps, on an island of Dominants, a woman who wasn't forward could find a man who would cherish her inexperience. Lizzie had to look on the bright side and cling to the hope that there must be a man, a Dom, on this island for her, even just for a night. She didn't need bells and whistles and romance. She needed to be wanted, because she never really had been. Not by anyone.

And in the end, that was what hurt the most.

She had to ignore the whispers of her heart, because a part of her knew deep down that she'd been waiting for Solomon almost her whole life. Since the moment they'd first met almost thirteen years ago, Lizzie had secretly yearned for him to be the one.

In order to achieve her goal and entice a stranger, she decided she had to pull out all the stops with her outfit. This was an island where dominance and submission were the name of the game. Just because she'd never had sex didn't mean she was ignorant, or didn't know how to dress to impress. If she had to play at being a submissive to lose her virginity, so be it. That didn't bother her—in fact, she'd prefer to have the man take charge. Which was why her outfit defied convention. With her smaller stature, she really did look like a schoolgirl—albeit a rather indecent one. Her plaid skirt stopped just past her rump. Her midriff was bare. Her white blouse was unbuttoned and played peek-a-boo with her black lace bra, and it was tied off beneath her breasts.

Her stockings were smooth over her calves and ended an inch above her knees. And instead of loafers, she wore black stilettos.

Would they be uncomfortable? Sure. But they made her legs look killer, and would hopefully attract the attention she sought.

She'd styled her blonde hair into two pigtail braids, which fell over her shoulders. Then she added the finishing touch, sliding on the island cuffs which had been provided with her room information. The smooth, supple leather was cool against her skin. She adjusted them so they wouldn't obstruct her hands or arms while she performed. Apparently, these puppies designated her as available to all the Dominants on the island. With these, she could kick her virginity to the curb. And if her heart ached at the thought that it wouldn't be Solomon doing the honors, she ignored it.

Lizzie left the bedroom with her music and flute case. On her way out the door, she spied her robe in the corner where she'd tossed it. She'd have to burn the thing, because she'd never wear it again.

SOLOMON SAT at the piano bench, cursing his very existence. At least his skull didn't still feel like it had been split in two. Granted, it was only marginally better, and his hangover had put him in a foul mood. He couldn't believe he'd passed out on the lounge chair and had woken up at dawn. More like he'd jolted awake at the incessant seagulls as they'd squawked over their morning meal and made him wish for someone to put him out of his misery.

Breakfast, ibuprofen, and a long steaming shower had helped burn off some of the alcohol and subsequent hangover. It had been years since he'd drunk too much. His dad had over-imbibed frequently and that had caused problems, so Solomon tended to avoid alcohol—and when he didn't, would only allow himself a few drinks. Not the entire effin' bottle.

His mission was to endure today: seeing Lizzie and not

wanting her with every fiber of his being. They had to return to their relationship prior to last night. It was the only way he'd survive this week without doing something they would both regret in the end. As he showered and readied himself for the day, he promised himself that tonight, he would make himself forget—not by drowning his sorrows in alcohol, which he usually never did—but by finding a willing sub in the club and losing himself in the moment. He was focused on the keys beneath his fingertips when Lizzie arrived in the alcove that served as their stage.

Her lavender scent washed over him and, instead of calming him, he realized his body was instantly alert at her proximity. When he was finally confident he could look at her without the ever-present hunger he felt whenever she was near, he lifted his head… and was drop-kicked in the solar plexus at the knock-out vision she presented.

Fuck me.

He gritted his teeth.

Need tore at his defenses. She was dressed like his every submissive fantasy brought to life. Solomon clenched his fists. He had to, otherwise he would yank her onto his lap and the hard ridge of his cock. Then they would give the guests at Pleasure Island a music show of a different variety. One where the only sounds were Lizzie's moans played in stereo sound and the slapping of flesh against flesh as he pounded inside her.

Incensed, fighting for his vaulted restraint, he snapped, "What the hell are you about, Lizzie? This isn't funny anymore."

With more control than he thought her capable of, she gave him a bland, doe-eyed stare as she said, "I don't know what you're talking about, Sol. I'm here to perform and that's it."

Sure she was, and he was the fucking Tooth Fairy. Suspicion laced his voice as he asked, "Then why are you dressed like, like a—"

"A submissive?" she murmured, a golden eyebrow raised, her lips pursed into a bow.

"Yes," he snarled, nearly biting his tongue off at the unbidden image of placing open-mouthed kisses over her exposed belly. Attaching the loops of her leather handcuffs above her head so she'd be unable to stop him. He shifted on the piano bench to ease his aching, straining erection.

"Well, I figured this was a good way to find a Dom who wants me. Shall we get started?" she asked, pulling her flute from its case and arranging her music on the nearby stand as if she was preparing for afternoon tea instead of looking like the epitome of submissive, downright fuckable perfection.

How was it that he was the one floundering while she appeared calm and collected? And she was, without a single effin' doubt, the most desirable woman of his acquaintance. He inhaled a few calming breaths. Solomon could accomplish this feat. Endure their performances today without cracking or giving in to his desire for her. When she bent over to pick up a sheet of music that had slipped to the ground, he almost came in his pants. She was wearing itty bitty black lace bikini panties that rode high on her butt cheeks beneath the plaid, barely-there skirt. The translucent round globes of her rear were just begging for his hands, entreating him to part the smooth flesh, slip aside the sheer black lace with a flick of his fingers, and slide his cock home until he was balls-deep inside her.

An image of Lizzie lying broken and in tears, pain radiating from her doe eyes, washed over him and acted like a bucket of cold water being dumped over his head. He wasn't for her. She was a grown woman—who looked like sin, but it wasn't his place to tell her what to wear or whom to be with. He was her friend. It was time he started acting like it.

"I'm ready. Let's begin." He redirected his focus to the keys and music, pouring his anguish and his need into every note.

Solomon ignored the other Doms' appreciative glances as

they blatantly caressed Lizzie. He disregarded the fact that she took his breath away when she performed. Passion exuded from her every pore. The music she played put her essence on display for the world to see. It didn't surprise him that there were Doms in the audience who gazed at her with rapt hunger. He understood the feeling all too well. Jared was standing off to one side, watching their performance. The hour flew by and then it was over.

Jared approached after the applause had erupted and people began to disperse. But not before Sol noticed the interested glances in the other Doms' faces as they obviously considered approaching Lizzie.

"Elizabeth, lass, don't you make a picture. I'm sure that after that performance, you will have them eating out of your hand this evening in the club," Jared said, giving her a friendly side arm hug.

"You think so?" Lizzie asked, a tremulous smile on her face.

And Solomon felt his heart stop at the naked hope in her voice. Then unfettered anger seethed and his blood rushed into his ears. Had last night been a game to her? If that was the case, Solomon would give her the fucking spanking she deserved for toying with his emotions like that.

"I do. You look most fetching. If you'd like me to introduce you to a few Doms who might suit you, I would be happy to do so, lass, as I know they are strangers to you."

"Really? I would love that," she replied.

Oh, she would, would she? Sol ground his teeth and kept his retort to himself. His temper simmered and boiled, needing an outlet before it exploded. Perhaps a quick run along the beach would burn it up.

Jared glanced his way and said, "Solomon, well done. Especially considering I heard you had a rather rough night."

Lizzie's gaze whipped to his, searching his face. And what would she see? That as long as they'd been friends, he'd wanted her with a fierceness even he himself didn't quite understand. She was the opposite of everything he looked for in a submissive and yet not one of the women he'd enticed into his bed had ever moved him the way she did. That even now, a part of him wished he'd said to hell with it last night, and buried himself in her warmth until he had fucked her out of his system. But he'd held himself back, for her.

The way Lizzie looked at him, though, the worry for him in her jade depths, scored him.

"It wasn't as bad as it sounds. And I'm fine now," Sol lied through his teeth and gave Jared a passive, hopefully convincing smirk.

"Yes, well, let me know if there's an issue that needs to be addressed. I'll be in my office if you need me. Lass, I will find you after the last show and escort you into the club."

"Thank you so much. I really do appreciate it," Lizzie murmured. Then she glanced at Solomon, her face unreadable for once. Normally her eyes told him everything he needed to know but right now, she kept her feelings hidden.

"So, this rough night of yours, want to tell me why?" Her alto voice was soft, slipping through his defenses and he shivered, feeling the haunting loveliness of it along his spine.

"I'm fine. Nothing to worry about," he assured her as he stood, escape on his mind. Solomon needed a breather from her. Otherwise, he couldn't be held responsible for his actions.

"Are you sure?" she asked, her gaze searching his face.

It was the spark of hope glimmering in her eyes that twisted his gut and punched a hole through his chest. Lizzie was killing him with her dewy glances and soft lips. He scowled and snapped, "Why wouldn't I be?"

She visibly flinched and murmured, "My mistake."

Then she walked away from him before he could stop her. And he let her leave. They had a two-hour break before their next show, and he needed the time to pull himself together. He had to be resolved in this: Solomon was not right for Lizzie. He was doing her a favor by cutting the possibility off at the knees, even if she didn't understand why. While he realized he should explain his actions to her—that was what any good friend would do—he worried that she would talk him out of his stance. She had that power over him and didn't even know it. He was thankful for that small miracle in the sea of shit he was currently treading water in.

No matter how much he wished that he didn't need to dissuade her and convince her that there was no chance or reality in which Solomon could take her to bed, that wasn't the case, and it never would be.

Chapter 6

After the last six months, what with breaking off her engagement and getting the cold shoulder from her parents, Lizzie believed she had experienced rock bottom with her emotions. That nothing else would be quite as painful as discovering her fiancé mid-coitus. Or having her parents, who'd never necessarily been the warmest people to begin with, shut her out of their lives. All because she refused to remain in said engagement so they could merge their assets with his family's.

Fine, *they* could marry the rotten bastard and leave her out of it. Which was what she'd told them. Hence the reason why her parents weren't presently speaking to her.

But she had been so wrong. The pain of those experiences was a mere fraction of what she had gone through over the last twenty-four hours. Today had been an exercise in torture. In theory, she'd hoped that once Solomon saw her dressed that way, he would cave like someone on a diet in an ice cream shop. Instead, she'd received a multitude of admiring glances from single Doms in attendance but not once did she get a heated reaction from the one man she yearned for with a ferocious anguish.

Nope, not her best friend. Solomon glared and judged, but gave nothing away as to his feelings. His unyielding silence and furious glances caused cracks to appear in her composure. Was the man made of stone? Did he hate her now? As much as they needed to discuss what had happened the previous night and repair the damage, Solomon's attitude was making any attempt at meaningful discussion untenable. At least for today.

Lizzie had never before been so relieved to have a day of performances finished. There was no way she'd be able to endure another day like this one. And she didn't know how to change the situation. The rift between her and Solomon growing by the minute. The very tangible fear that things between her and Solomon would never be repaired, especially with him avoiding her, was steadily increasing.

Lizzie had made a mess of their friendship. She knew it was all on her, and couldn't fathom how to go about correcting it.

Jared joined her then, with a stunning beauty at his side. Her skin was the color of molten caramel and dark ebony curls framed her face. The bright, fire-engine red halter dress hugged her curves. She was short in stature, like Lizzie, but that was where the similarity ended. She was much more well-endowed in hip and definitely in bust, making Lizzie feel more like a teenage boy with her small cleavage.

"Elizabeth, I'd like you to meet my Naomi," Jared said, introducing the raven-haired beauty at his side with such love and devotion in his gaze, jealousy swamped Lizzie. She couldn't help it. The emotions Jared obviously held for his fiancée were what she had prayed she would find with Solomon. It was like a knife through the chest, and Lizzie almost wavered in her mission to see the end of her virgin state.

Naomi gave her a shy smile and said, "You play so beautifully. The show was wonderful, truly."

"Thank you. It's so nice to meet you finally. I'm thrilled that Jared invited me. The island is a perfect getaway." Lizzie smiled, determined to cover up her sorrow if it killed her.

"You will be joining us for dinner on Thursday, yes?" Naomi asked.

"That would be just lovely. If there's anything I can do to help you out in the kitchen, please let me know."

At the dark, male snort behind her, Lizzie cringed inwardly. "What Lizzie has so conveniently forgotten is that she can't even boil water without burning it."

"I may not be a good cook, but I can help decorate, carry, and clean-up," she defended herself, giving Solomon a sideways glare. Sol had been in the kind of mood today that made a pool of hungry sharks seem more appealing. He'd bitten her head off for the slightest error. Regarded her with stony silences and furious glowers. How could she breach the walls of his defenses to apologize when he fired barbs at every turn?

"Are you ready to go to the club, Elizabeth, or do you need a minute?" Jared asked, his arm around Naomi's waist, holding her in a possessive, protective manner that made Lizzie sigh internally. To have someone who wanted to touch her, a man who would hold her and proclaim to the world that she belonged with him—she wanted it so fiercely, with a stark yearning that ached. It was the one thing she'd always wanted, to have someone she belonged to who wanted her, not for money or power, but because they couldn't imagine being without her, and craved who she was and who she would be, lauded her victories and comforted her after defeats. That had been Solomon once—all but the possessiveness and holding her—but still, him and their friendship.

Was she ready for the club? As she would ever be. It was time. No more stalling or delaying what must occur. Maybe once she had lost this infernal title, she could put the need for a physical relationship to rest and focus on rebuilding her friendship with Solomon. But Lizzie needed a moment to herself first. She'd been surrounded all day during her performances. She said, "Well, I need to take my instrument back up to my room. Then I am."

"Understood. Would you like us to wait for you down here, lass, or prefer to meet us in the club? Your choice," Jared offered.

"Why don't you both go ahead and I will meet you there. I don't want to hold you up and this should only take a few minutes," Lizzie said. She would have more peace of mind if she had a few minutes longer to gather her composure.

"I can see that she gets there in one piece, Jared," Solomon offered, his expression giving nothing away. Jared seemed to have a sixth sense about him; his glance shifted between them. Lizzie used every ounce of strength she possessed to appear calm and composed, when just the opposite was true.

"That's good then." Jared nodded and steered Naomi through the lobby.

Lizzie followed with Solomon at her back. Unease infused her. Why was Sol being so accommodating in escorting her to her room? She hated that she was suddenly suspicious of his motives. But she couldn't help it. He'd been snarling at her all day. Not that she blamed him exactly, but he was acting like an ass instead of her best friend. The four of them rode the elevator together. The lift stopped at the club level, where Jared and Naomi exited. "See you in a few minutes. Come join me on the far dais, lass, and I will introduce you to some fine Doms I believe would suit."

"I will. Thank you," Lizzie responded. This was what she wanted. It might not be with whom she wanted, but that seemed to be the story of her life. She always had to be satisfied with something or someone else.

As soon as the elevator doors slid shut, Solomon pounced like he'd been lying in wait, and backed Lizzie up against the wall of the lift. His countenance screamed fury and some darker emotion she couldn't quite place. His hands caged her body in, flat against the wall as he leaned close. His exotic scent washed over her, liquid pulls of heat swirled in her core.

He frowned, a muscle ticked in his jaw, and his voice was low, dangerous in its tenor. "What the fuck, Lizzie? I thought you were hot under the collar for me. At least that was what you insinuated with your little strip tease last night. But you've done an about face and plan to throw yourself at any Dom who waves his dick in your direction?"

His words sliced her soul into ribbons. It took everything inside her not to put her hands on him. Solomon was so close, a hair's breadth away. If she leaned forward a mere inch, their bodies would align from hip to shoulder. She almost dared, almost pushed Solomon to react one way or another. A part of her believed that if she touched him, kissed him again, he wouldn't be able to deny her. But the fury in his gunmetal eyes stalled her actions and she wilted against the wall, trying to put distance between them. She said, unable to hide her sorrow, "That's none of your concern now, is it? You said no rather clearly last night, and that we were to forget it ever happened. Or do you not remember?"

Solomon glowered, his eyes simmered with unspoken heat, and a corresponding ache burned within her soul. He muttered low, his words caressing her, "I remember everything about last night. But I can't seem to wrap my brain around the fact that you could move so quickly from wanting me to deciding to fuck another man. This isn't you, Lizzie, and you know it."

"Well, clearly you have no idea what I need, Sol. Otherwise we wouldn't be having this conversation." She clamped her lips shut. If she said anymore, she'd look like a bloody fool.

The doors slid open with a soft ding, her freedom a short distance away.

"Now, if you will excuse me, I have plans this evening." When he didn't move right away, she ducked beneath his arms and exited the lift. Her feet moved swiftly, her heels clicking as she strode hurriedly down the hall, needing the space.

For a moment back there, she'd thought he meant to kiss her. She shook her head as she opened the door to her room, shutting it behind her as she heard Solomon's door open and then slam shut. It had been wishful thinking on her part. Lizzie had done everything she could to tempt him into wanting her. The cold hard truth was that he didn't. She had to accept it as fact and move on. It was time she built the life she chose.

She laid her flute case and folder of sheet music on the coffee table. What a mess. Lizzie couldn't remember ever feeling this lost before. She'd depended upon Solomon to have her back. She had since they'd first met. At the thought of that comfort and support vanishing, anguish washed over her and nearly brought her to her knees. How was she supposed to live without him?

That was the question which had kept her up last night. She hated that she had caused the rift between them. Would he despise her after tonight?

She clutched her hand against her chest, attempting to rub the ache away. But it was too deep-seated. Swiping at the wetness coating her lashes, she grimaced. As if she didn't have enough issues, now she'd gone and smudged her makeup. Blowing out a frustrated breath, Lizzie trudged into the bathroom to freshen up. Even if her heart was bleeding, she'd never show it. She'd learned that if you let people see your weaknesses, they tended to attack like vultures, ripping a body to shreds.

As she fixed her makeup, she knew there was only one course of action she could take. Solomon wasn't an option. If Jared had Doms he wanted to introduce her to, she would play along. She yearned to be rid of her virgin status far too much. Lizzie craved physical contact. She had everything else quite literally at her feet, except in this one regard, and beggars couldn't be choosy.

Besides, if any of them were the men who'd attended her

performances today, she might be in for a treat. There had been plenty of attractive guys in their ranks.

She finished retouching her makeup, then used the facilities. Lizzie prayed that she would be able to convince whoever did the honors tonight to take her back to their room for the festivities. She really didn't want her first time to have an audience. But if needs must, then so be it.

She didn't have butterflies in her belly but stampeding bulls as she left her room and retraced her steps back to the bank of elevators. Pride swelled in her chest that she didn't once glance over her shoulder and stare at the door to Solomon's room. She used that to bolster her spirits, and plastered a smile on her face. Inside she might feel like curling up in the fetal position, but outwardly she looked fabulous and on top of the world. The ride down was so much smoother than the one up, without Solomon's potent energy pervading the space.

When the elevator halted, Lizzie emerged into the club. Music thumped loudly from hidden speakers. The elegance of the hotel extended to the Dungeon Club. The furniture was large and masculine. The leather couches and chairs were midnight black, the kind a body could sink into, with hidden silver loops spaced at varying intervals. Continuing the semi gothic urbanite flare, the wall bar was sleek, glossy black, and lined the wall on the right. The club was packed already for the night, the golden lighting dim, giving the place a haunting quality as she moved deeper into the lair of sexual decadence. Many of the couches and barstools were occupied. With the number of alpha Doms in attendance, the testosterone levels were off the charts.

Lizzie glanced at the faces of the Doms she passed, wondering who among them would be the one for tonight. There was sex furniture in the alcoves that resembled tiny gray stone dungeons, many of which already contained couples getting their freak on. Lizzie hated to admit that the lifestyle fascinated her. Winding her way through the crowd, she spied Jared with Naomi in his lap, reclining on a throne as he kept an eye on the festivities. On shaky legs she approached, wondering who he had selected for her.

"Elizabeth, lass, I see that you finally decided to join us tonight. I was beginning to wonder if you chose to stay in your room instead."

"No, Sir," she said, remembering how she was supposed to address a Dom while in the club.

"Well, have a seat," he murmured, and indicated a small, cushioned chair beside his throne. The seat was lower than his, which forced her to crane her neck a bit if she wanted to speak with him. Lizzie's inexperience made her feel like she stuck out, as if everyone in the place was waiting for her to make a faux pas.

Once she was seated, a waitress wearing even less than she was approached them on the small, raised stage.

"Can I get you anything to drink, Master Jared? Would your sub like anything?" she asked, her vibrant, cherry red curls shifting around her small shoulders.

"I'll have a Guinness, Samantha, bring a chardonnay for Naomi. Elizabeth, what would you prefer?"

"A glass of cabernet would be lovely, thank you," she replied. The liquid courage would help her out quite a bit and settle her nerves. The last thing she wanted was to have a Dom touch her and she end up jumping away from him. It would put a bit of a crink in her desire to get laid. Her gaze moved over the crowd and shuddered to a halt. Solomon sat on one of the barstools, his dark and foreboding gaze more intent than a tiger about to strike. He was wearing form-fitting leather pants and a tank. Did he have to look so gorgeous? It was like the man was trying to spite her.

Their waitress returned with their drinks, thank the maker.

"And the cab for Elizabeth," Samantha murmured, handing her the wine glass.

Lizzie accepted the offering and replied, "Thank you."

Samantha nodded with a small smile but looked to Jared, or Master Jared, as he was called here. She had to remember that little tidbit. Lizzie swallowed a few sips of wine.

"Thank you, Samantha lass, we are good for now," Jared said, sounding like a king in his domain.

"Yes, Sir," Samantha replied and moved silently away, off to her next set of patrons.

Lizzie mainlined her wine—the first half—like they were going to run out. Warmth spread throughout her body and she felt herself relax some. With Solomon glaring daggers at her, that wasn't an easy feat to accomplish. Jared shifted Naomi in his lap and regarded her. "You seem unsettled. Is there a problem? I've never seen you at one of the clubs. While you definitely look like a sub, why am I getting a different vibe off you, lass?"

Lizzie grimaced internally. Of course he would know. Jared always seemed to know everything, like he was psychic or something, or just inherently good at reading people. How much to say? Certainly not: 'Well gee, Master Jared, I'm a virgin and don't want to be anymore.' That would not go over well. She answered as honestly as possible. "No, there's no problem. I'm just new to the lifestyle and still uncomfortable with everything being out in the open. I prefer my interactions behind closed doors."

Jared studied her for a moment, like he was seeing past her defenses to her core being, past the false pretenses to the lies she'd wrapped around her personage. "It's good that you told me. It does narrow down who I think would be a good fit for you."

As long as she still had choices, that was fine by her. "I will trust your judgement on this, being that I don't know anyone here."

Approval swam in his gaze and he nodded. "Very good. How do you feel about two Doms at once?"

"Two?" she asked, glad she hadn't just taken a drink. She sucked in air and couldn't stop her heart palpitations. Two men to help rid her of her virginity? Now that was an introduction to sex if there ever was one. Could she do it, be brave enough?

"If that's too much for you, you need to let me know now. The owner of Underworld out in New Orleans, Michael, and his pal, Dante, enjoy topping subs together and mentioned an interest. I think they, more than the other available Doms on the island, would suit you. Would you like an introduction?"

The stampede had returned, but she nodded. "Yes, Sir, I would."

What the hell! Life was short and she was ready. Lizzie wanted to get this show on the road. The sooner it was done with, the sooner she could move on and stop feeling like she was walking around with a scarlet letter on her chest, proclaiming to all the world that she was a virgin.

Jared signaled someone with his gaze and she followed his line of sight. The duo in question approached. She'd seen them earlier at the second performance today. They were a study in contrasts. One light and golden, the other dark and foreboding, and the alpha animal magnetism of each Dom was a living breathing entity. Their heated gazes made her skin feel like it was three sizes too small. That was a good thing, right? It meant she was feeling some desire for them.

Although, if truth be told, Lizzie would have to be dead not to feel something. They were sexy, and sinfully gorgeous. Their eyes held a sensual knowledge as they looked her over—like they'd already stripped her in their minds and found her to their liking.

Jared stood, and held out a hand to Lizzie. She accepted and rose to her feet, the wine glass gripped in her free hand like a lifeline, and praying they couldn't see her anxiety. Jared said, "Gentlemen, I would like to introduce you to Elizabeth. Lass, this is Dante and Michael."

It was the blond Adonis who reached her first. His eyes were as deep a blue as the water beyond the island, his hair was a few shades darker blond than hers, and long like Jared's, reaching his shoulders. His angular jaw was dusted with a short beard, expertly trimmed, and made his already full lips appear delectable. Those same lips were spread in an easy, enticing grin meant to seduce. And holy moly, he was tall. Towering over her, he was taller than Jared and Solomon—who were both big men —with shoulders like a linebacker's. His voice was smooth and well-cultured, with a hint of a southern drawl as he said, "Elizabeth, my friend Dante and I would enjoy the pleasure of your company this evening. Would you like to come sit with us and get to know us better?"

Dante was nearly as large as Michael, perhaps an inch or so shorter, his shoulders nearly as broad, but that was where any similarity between them ended. Where Michael was golden-skinned and golden-haired, Dante was dark. His hair was black as midnight, long enough for an enterprising woman to slide her hand through and artfully arranged to appear disheveled. His intense eyes were like molten dark chocolate with dark upturned brows slashed above them. His mouth was fuller, more sensual than Michael's. His square jaw was covered in perpetual dark stubble and his skin deeply tanned. Inky black tattoos covered his shoulders and disappeared beneath his tank.

Could she handle this much testosterone in one sitting? Between the two of them, they outweighed her by three hundred pounds, easily, and looked like pure, undiluted alpha males bent on seduction. Lizzie couldn't contain her tremors any more. She opened her mouth to reply and Jared interceded. "She is uncomfortable with public displays yet, and is new to the lifestyle. I give you both my consent as long as her wish to use one of the private rooms is respected."

It was Dante who spoke then, quirking a dark slash of raised brow. "A newly christened submissive? Have you ever been with two men, my sweet?"

"No, Sir. But I would enjoy getting to know you both." She lowered her gaze, her voice barely an audible whisper, and caught Solomon's grim stare. It was like a dagger through her heart. There was nothing for it. The two men in front of her actually wanted her. They were her course now and she wouldn't back down from it.

"Then come, sit with us and we will do just that, Elizabeth," Michael said, a sound of deep pleasure rumbling in his massive chest.

"Please call me Lizzie, Sirs," she murmured, and accepted Michael's outstretched hand. His enormous fingers closed around hers, dwarfing them. Her breath backed up into her throat at the contact. They were going to touch a whole lot more before the night was over. Michael towed her forward, away from the dais, and Dante flanked her other side. He slid a massive, thick arm around her waist, and she shivered at the possessive touch. Michael and Dante claimed one of the vacant couches in order to accommodate the three of them.

They sandwiched her between their big, hard bodies on the smooth black leather that was butter soft to the touch. Heat emanated from them, so much so it felt like she was surrounded by her own personal space heaters. She couldn't deny how uber feminine they made her feel, being the center of their combined attention. The only downside, and it was like a damn Greek tragedy, was that the couch they were seated on faced the bar, very close to the one person she wanted to avoid tonight. One glance at Solomon and she knew she had to ignore him if she was going to accomplish why she was there that evening.

"What was it about the lifestyle that attracted you?" Michael asked, jolting her attention away from Solomon. She shifted her gaze up to Michael's. He was handsome in a classic way, the sort of guy you'd expect to grace a magazine cover, but there was a carnal eroticism in his blue eyes that let her know he was up for anything in the pleasure department.

"Because I always have to be in control of everything, and it's the one place I don't want to be." Which was at least true. Whenever she had fantasized about sex—and lately she had, quite a bit—she wanted to give up her control and let the man be in charge. The fact that she always imagined it was Solomon was a moot point.

"Many woman, especially those in business or at the top of their field, tend to enjoy giving up control in the bedroom. So you're not unusual, though I do find you fascinating. It's rare to come across such an untried beauty as yourself, and one as passionate as you are," Michael said.

"But how do you know that, Sir? If you don't mind my asking."

"Not at all." Michael smiled then, a wealth of knowledge in his gaze. "It's there for all to see when you perform, love. Your heart, the passion you hold within you, is in every note you play. And it's quite intoxicating. You make a Dom want to be the one who gets the privilege of being with you, the one to draw it out of you and give it back to you tenfold."

"Oh, well, um…" She didn't know what to say to that and heat permeated her cheeks.

"We both saw it, my sweet. How long have you played the flute professionally? Have you ever been to New Orleans?" Dante asked, and she shifted her gaze to his.

"Yes, I've been playing most of my life. I attended Julliard and have played with symphonies all around the world. And yes, I've been to New Orleans and the French Quarter. I don't know if I could live there, because the food is so spectacular I would want to eat all the time, but it's a lovely city, Sirs."

"The next time you are in town, I insist you visit my club there, Underworld. My place would suit you, if you've a mind to it," Michael said, teasing her nape with his hand, toying with her braids. She felt his touch all the way to her toes. It wasn't quite like the earth-shattering explosions Solomon's touch wrought, but her body warmed to Michael's hypnotic touch.

"Well, now, my sweet, do you have any hard limits Mike and I should know about?" Dante purred, tracing his fingers above her stockings. Shivers erupted along her spine from his touch. And she realized that the questions had all been to put her at ease and make her feel comfortable with them. Perhaps, if she knew what to expect, she might, but as it was, every sensation was new to her. Would they be mad at her for not telling them the truth? Would they turn away from her, cast her out, and tell Jared? She knew it was risky to hide it from them.

As Michael's fingers caressed the flesh beneath one of her braids, she jumped.

"Easy, love," Michael murmured, his mouth dangerously close to her ear. "You need not fear us. We only wish to bring you unabashed pleasure tonight. And we won't adjourn to a private room until you feel confident that you want to spend the night with us."

Dante's firm hand slid beneath her skirt, his fingers grazed her inner thigh, and she gasped. "About those limits, sweet, hmm?"

"Yes, right, sorry, Sir. I haven't tried much so I'm not certain. If that's an issue, and you don't want me tonight because of it, I'll understand and I won't hold it against you." She lowered her lashes, praying that they wouldn't turn her away. She couldn't withstand any more rejection from men. That seemed to be all she'd ever experienced, and she'd developed a bit of a complex over. And, well, who wouldn't?

"Hmmm, you're that new to our lifestyle?" Michael asked, turning her face toward him. He looked like an avenging angel with his shoulder-length blond hair and blue eyes.

If they only knew the truth—and would know relatively soon

just how new to the lifestyle she was, to sex in general. She said, "Yes, Sir, I am."

"Well, if you're game, my sweet, we promise to make it worth your while," Dante growled and laid an open-mouthed kiss on her exposed shoulder.

She gasped as Michael rasped his thumb over her bottom lip and his partner cupped her breast through her bra, teasing her nipple through the lace.

"So what's it to be? Should we head into one of the private rooms?" Michael queried, his gaze searching her face.

This was it, she was going to do it. She licked her dry lips and said, "Yes, Sirs. I would like that very much."

Michael's blue gaze darkened with desire and he lowered his mouth to hers. At the first touch of his lips as they hungrily brushed against hers, deep down, Lizzie understood that while Michael was a gorgeous man and the night ahead might even be memorable, her body didn't respond to his the way it did to Solomon's. But it had to be enough. Needing to prove it to herself, she returned Michael's kiss as he pressed his thumb against her jaw, opening her mouth wider so he could plunge his tongue inside to duel with hers.

At the sharp bite against her nipple, she mewled into Michael's mouth as pleasure spiked in her veins and lanced directly to her sex. Between her thighs, her pussy throbbed and she wanted Dante's fingers to close the distance and touch her intimate flesh. Strike her previous thought about it not being passionate enough. The two men together were going to equal Solomon. They would wipe that one kiss from her recollection, and she welcomed the thought.

"I want a taste," Dante growled, his hand at her chin, turning her gaze to his own black, hungry one. Then his firm lips pressed against hers while Michael stroked his hands over her body.

This could really work for her. Her body became fluid under their expert hands. The sooner they could get to the private room, the better. She'd be able to claim 'mission accomplished' within the hour.

"That's enough, Lizzie, you've had your fun. It's time to stop now." Solomon's furious and deadly voice penetrated their heated exchange.

Both Dante and Michael stilled. Dante released her lips and scowled at him.

"Find your own damn sub. This one's ours tonight," Dante said, his voice firm, brooking no room for argument.

"Actually, that one is mine. Lizzie belongs to me. She's pissed at me right now, and I let her act out so I could see how far she would take it. Now it's gone further than I'm willing to allow. Take your fucking hands off my sub," Solomon snarled at Michael and Dante, his fists clenched. The thunderous glare he aimed in Lizzie's direction chilled her, like he was daring her to argue with him. She didn't understand what was happening. Why was he doing this to her? Hadn't he done enough with his callous disregard?

"Is this true?" Michael growled, his eyes narrowed, his face no longer warm and inviting but downright livid.

"I don't know what he's talking about. He didn't want me," Lizzie spat, shaking. She was so furious with Solomon, she wanted to throttle him into next week. How dare he wreck her carefully laid plans? First he said he wasn't the man for her, and then he intervened when she tried to find ones who *did* want her. What was wrong with him? Did he simply hate her and want to make her life a living hell?

"It seems the lady is telling a different tale." Dante's hand still caressed her, running over her flesh in a soothing manner.

"Like I said before, she's angry with me. But she's my sub. I can describe her body explicitly, right down to where she has a tiny, heart-shaped mole. You will take your hands off her this instant and find some other one who suits. There are plenty enough for you here," Sol said.

"But we want this one. She came to us willingly and is wearing the cuffs that proclaim to all and sundry that she's a free agent," Michael murmured. His voice sounded calm but was laced with steel.

Jared intervened then, standing between Solomon and the two Doms flanking her. He asked, his glance assessing the situation, "Is there a problem?"

"There is," Solomon vehemently admitted, his usual staunch, stoic control conspicuously absent. "Lizzie is, in fact, my sub. She's angry with me and trying to torment me, like she always does. I was willing to see how far she was planning to push it, because I tend to enjoy punishing her sweet ass, but she crossed the line when she agreed to be with these two and head to a private room."

So he'd been listening to their entire exchange. Why? Lizzie's heart couldn't handle all the yo-yoing back and forth. Did this mean Sol had lied last night and did want her? If so, then why had he turned her away like that? Why did he break her heart?

"Elizabeth, lass, is what Solomon's saying true?" Jared asked, his gaze intent, obviously attempting to divine the truth. She had four pairs of furious Dom eyes studying her. Michael and Dante were no longer stroking and caressing her flesh—they could have been statues for all their movement. But it was Solomon who garnered her wrath. Tears, which she normally could hide, sprang into the corners of her eyes and coated her lashes. And she knew how that made her look—guilty—as though Solomon were the injured party.

"If that's the case, lass, then you will be punished. I do not take lightly to my rules being so blatantly broken," Jared said. His expression had changed; the gentle kindness she'd seen not twenty minutes prior had been replaced by an apparently immovable, stern Dom.

Anger vibrated through her. What the hell did a girl have to do to freaking get laid? And now she had the two men who were, just mere seconds ago, willing and able, glaring at her. Jared's face was like granite. And as for Solomon—she wanted to beat him across the head with her flute and would have, if it were nearby.

"You're all assholes!" Lizzie jumped to her feet and, with as much finesse as possible in those damn stupid heels that made her feet ache, attempted to storm past the group. None of them expected that outburst from her, which was why she made it as far as she did.

"And you're the biggest asshole of them all," she snarled at Solomon and tried to shove past him. The man confounded her. She had no idea why he'd humiliate her like this. Escape was the only thing on her mind; she had to leave before the sob lodged in her throat was expelled. She felt like a wounded, trapped animal, ready to lash out at the nearest person. Why did people use her like this? Play with her emotions?

"It's clear to us, she is definitely yours. We don't normally poach on another Dom's territory," Michael murmured behind her, and she winced. Before she could make it past Solomon, Jared caught her arm. His hand was akin to steel manacles surrounding her bicep.

"You will be punished. House rules. And since Dante and Michael are the injured party here, lass, they will get to decide your punishment," Jared said, looking every inch the Master of this club. Her heart sank and she wondered what further degradation she would be forced to endure before the nightmare ended. Was she supposed to be the one who was never touched? Never held? Never loved?

"No one lays a finger on my sub, punishment or no. I will see to it that she is disciplined. And if you don't like it, we will leave at first light," Solomon threatened.

Lizzie whipped her glance to his, attempting to decipher his meaning.

"Clearly, these two have issues they need to work out. I'm fine with him disciplining his sub as recompense. From the looks of it, she won't sit pretty for a week," Dante interjected, leaning back against the couch.

"I agree," Michael said, but his voice, which had been so full of fire and promise of passion, was flat.

Jared released her arm, his gaze hard. "Fine, but she will not be allowed back in the Dungeon Club until she's been properly disciplined."

Like Lizzie would come back here. It was just another clusterfuck in a whole series of them in her life. She wasn't planning to come back to relive her humiliation any time soon. She wondered whether staying on the island and following through with her commitment to perform was even worth it. Maybe she should just back out of the contract and leave on the first ferry out. She had more than enough money to pay recompense to Jared for breaking the contract. Solomon didn't need her to perform. He could give concerts all by his lonesome, without doing a duet with her.

And then Solomon's hand slid around her bicep, a prison more daunting than the walls of Alcatraz. She seemed to have traded one jailor for another, but this one dragged her from the club. All eyes were riveted on them and the drama spectacle they created. Ignoring the furious glares of the Doms they passed, she held her head high. She'd not done a damn thing wrong, even though they weren't aware of that. The whole trip so far had been a bust, much like the rest of her life. It shouldn't surprise her that it had all gone to hell in a hand basket faster than she could blink. What she didn't know, was why.

She was seething, ready to claw Solomon's eyes out the moment they were alone. He talked about playing games. Well, who was playing them now?

Chapter 7

Lizzie didn't speak as they rode the elevator up, nor when they disembarked and he tugged her down the hall.

Solomon hauled her into his room. The moment the door was shut, she whirled on him. Her rage exploded. She shoved against his chest. "What the fuck is wrong with you? Huh? Do you get off on making me miserable? How dare you?"

She pushed at his chest again for further emphasis. Not that it did much good. The man was more solid than a mountain, and impossible to move.

"Are you done?" Solomon asked, his voice deadly calm. His eyes blazed but he held himself still, all controlled, stern alpha Dom.

Asshole. His attitude infuriated her.

Lizzie wasn't sure why but his cool restraint made her snap. All the humiliations, all the pain and agony she had suffered at the hands of others, suffocated her. Without thought of repercussions, her wrath fueled her actions and she beat her fists against his chest. Tears fell as she sobbed, "Why? I don't understand. You turned me down. I wanted you and you said no. And then the moment I seek out someone else, you act like you own me, embarrass me in front of everyone here. I won't be able to face any of them come morning. And it's all your fault."

And then she was sobbing into his chest, her face buried against him, her hands clutching him. It was the indignity of everything she'd suffered. Her ex-fiancé lying to her. The way he had pretended to care, to love her, that he wanted to wait to make love until they were married. The fact that she had allowed him to push back their wedding date because he 'just wasn't ready yet,' only to discover him in bed with another woman. And then for him to end up blaming her, saying that she was frigid for not seducing him and sleeping with him, as a good fiancée should.

And last, there was Solomon. The one man she'd always counted on. When he'd turned her away last night, a part of her felt like it had died. She'd already felt so unloved and unwanted by her parents and her ex… only to have Sol dismiss her as well. Lizzie feared who she would become if she wasn't allowed to be a normal woman and experience love and passion—one of those broken individuals whom people tended to look at with obvious pity in their eyes.

Lizzie didn't know what to do any more. Obviously there was something inherently wrong with her, something that was just unlovable, and she somehow lacked what everyone else seemed to get with ease.

When she realized she was clinging to Solomon, she shoved away—or tried to, at least.

Solomon's gaze had darkened and was unreadable in the dimly lit room.

"Let me go, Sol. Haven't you done enough for one night?" she said with a ragged sob.

"I can't. You got what you wanted. For this week, you're mine, Lizzie."

"You actually think after everything, after the stunts you pulled tonight, that you—that *we*—are going to have sex? You're barking mad, you know that? Off your rocker and ready for the asylum if you think I'm going to let you—"

He shut her up. With his mouth. He slanted his lips over hers and the fight simply evaporated from her bones. Lizzie's brain clicked off as he dominated her mouth. Solomon showed her, with more than words, that she was not only going to be with him, she was going to like it. This was what had been missing from Michael and Dante's kisses. Not that they had been horrible, but they weren't Solomon. The fire, the passion, and the way her bones melted as she leaned against him.

Her nails dug into his chest and she pressed her body against his. He commanded a response from her body, and that, damn traitor that it was, couldn't have been happier or more attuned to another man.

Lizzie felt alive for the very first time. Like she'd been experiencing life through a filtered lens before. Solomon knew exactly how to kiss. If he stopped now, like he had in Scotland, she'd do him physical harm. All the embarrassment of the last twenty-four hours simply melted away and was replaced with an inferno of need. She had no idea why he'd changed his mind. As long as he didn't stop kissing her, Lizzie didn't care.

This was Solomon. Her Solomon, kissing her into the freaking stratosphere.

Her hands slid beneath the cotton of his shirt of their own accord, and skimmed over his taut belly. Lizzie's fingers traced the lines of his six pack and happy trail. She whimpered against his mouth. She had to get closer, feel his naked skin against hers. Solomon growled against her mouth as she teased the waistband of his leather pants. In a move that left her breathless, he spun her around and pressed her back up against the door. They'd not made it further into the room than the freaking door.

Not breaking his domineering kiss, Solomon hoisted her into his arms. Instinct had her wrapping her legs around his waist. At the feel of his firm erection through the leather, intimately snug against her aching pussy, Lizzie moaned into his mouth. His hands tore her blouse in half, the rending of fabric joining her mewls in the room. His fingers unclasped her black lace bra, and only then did he release her mouth.

He stared at her breasts with unbridled hunger. She waited for him to move, breathing in short, shallow pants as need cascaded through her system.

With the barest touch, his fingers glided over her cleavage, caressing the hard points. Pleasure arced through her body and she moaned. "Please."

He chuckled darkly, not stopping his torture. "Just hold on to me, mia bella."

Then his mouth descended over one of the pert buds. At the first tug, she whimpered, and her head thunked back against the door. She moaned as he teased her skin, lashing his tongue against her nipple. Her fingers threaded into his black hair as he nibbled on the heart-shaped mole beneath her right breast. He nipped, he sucked, and Lizzie was going up in flames. A heightened awareness had suffused her limbs so that all she could feel was Solomon and his incredible mouth.

He placed open-mouthed kisses on the space between her breasts as he moved from one to the other. She became need. He touched her and she mewled. He closed his mouth over her flesh and she keened. He surrounded her, invading her every sense.

When he lowered her feet to the ground, she whined and then gasped as he crowded her body against the door and he knelt before her. He lifted her leg up and ripped the delicate lace of her panties so she was bare before him, the skirt shoved up to her waist. Then he arranged her thighs so her legs were spread wide to accommodate his broad shoulders; his mouth hovered over her pussy, and her legs dangled over his shoulders. He used the door for support and swiped his tongue through her folds.

"Oh god," she cried, her head falling back. His tongue was working magic on her most intimate flesh. Lizzie hadn't realized sex could be like this. She felt the first stirrings of her orgasm. She'd masturbated plenty, but this was so much more. Solomon feasted on her, circling her clit with his tongue, swiping it across her swollen bud in a series of fast flicks until she writhed and panted his name like a benediction.

"Sol," she screamed, and came around his tongue as he plunged it inside her slick heat. Trembling, quaking, she rode the waves of ecstasy. Her limbs were heavy, her eyes half-lidded. She groaned as he removed her legs from his shoulders and set them on the floor. And then Solomon stood, sliding up her body, keeping her upright with his strength. He yanked his tank off over his shoulders, tossed the offending garment behind him without a care for where it fell. Then his hands were at his leather pants, unbuttoning them and freeing his turgid shaft.

His cock was beautiful. Long and erect, the head smooth. She wanted to kiss the tip, taste the tiny drop of dew there. Lizzie wondered if he would let her. Then he was lifting her back into her arms, pulling her legs up to his waist. At the first contact of his manhood against her slick, puffy folds, she nearly lost her mind. He felt so good. She needed him. Now. She'd waited a lifetime for him.

A pained expression crossed his face. "Shit, I need a—"

No. She wasn't letting him go now. Not after everything. She rubbed herself against him, beyond the ability to wait any longer. She begged, "Please, Sol, now. I'm on the pill. Let me feel all of you inside me."

Lust shrouded his face and his chest rumbled with a guttural groan at her words. He gripped his member and fit the smooth crown at her entrance. Her gaze was locked on his as he thrust forward—and stopped when he encountered the tiny membrane barrier. His mouth dropped open.

He sputtered, a wealth of emotions flashing across his visage, "Lizzie, what the? How?"

"I know it will hurt at first, just do it. Please, I—"

"Fuck," he muttered and kissed her, covered her mouth with his, then he pushed through the thin membrane. Pain stole her breath and lanced through her as her body resisted his invasion. Solomon worked his shaft inside with gentle, smooth thrusts until his cock was embedded fully. She whimpered at the mix of pleasure and pain. He was so big, she didn't know how it would ever feel comfortable. But he held still, buried inside her, giving her body time to acclimate to his, and seduced her with his mouth. Made her focus on the incredible way his lips traveled over hers. He kissed her gently, sweetly distracting her. Then his hands cupped the back of her head to hold her steady as he plundered her depths with his tongue, seemingly touching her very soul before shifting to dominating, hungry kisses that stole the breath from her body.

Solomon kissed her until all the tension in her seemed to unwind. The discomfort behind the initial breach melted into a sea of profound and startling pleasure.

One of his big hands slid between them and he thrummed his fingers against her clit. His mouth never left hers as he stroked her tiny nub. Only when he'd brought her to orgasm again with his fingers, her sheath quaking and clasping around his cock, did Solomon begin to move again. With a roll of his hips, he thrust and withdrew. Her arms were around his shoulders, her nails digging into his back as he ground and plunged. His hands cupped her rear as he furrowed deep. Pleasure unlike anything she'd experienced before permeated every molecule of her being.

Experimentally, she writhed against him. With Sol, the movement felt as natural as breathing. He pumped his shaft inside her, his pace increasing bit by bit. She'd never felt so full or complete before. Where once she had been empty, now she overflowed with him. Her sheath clamped around his member as if her body was attempting to draw him deeper, make them one being.

Solomon broke their kiss, his gaze steady on hers as he

pounded, pressing her back against the door. It was like he was trying to become a part of her as he thrust. Her body coiled as she undulated her hips and, with a flick of Solomon's fingers across her clit, Lizzie shattered.

She screamed as she came. Her body vibrated and tears streamed from her eyes as she shook. Then Solomon's cock jerked inside her clenching heat. He strained as he pounded, roaring as he erupted, hot streams of his seed pouring inside her quivering sheath.

He buried his face in the hollow of her neck. His lips pressed against her skin. She rested her cheek against his head. Her eyes closed. Without his support, she'd be a puddle on the floor. She felt warm, and more satisfied than ever before.

He nipped the top of her shoulder and then lifted his face. His eyes were fierce. "Why didn't you tell me?"

"What?"

His gaze became infinitely tender. "That you were still a virgin."

With the freedom to touch him now like never before, she traced his jaw with her thumb, the pad scraping against his stubble. "Because you never would have touched me and I wanted you to, more than anything."

His eyes slid shut and an anguished expression crossed his face, but then the dratted man settled on anger. He growled, the rumble vibrating where their chests were meshed together. "I'll touch you, all right. After the stunts you've pulled in the last twenty-four hours, I'm going to do what I should have done last night."

"I thought you already did," she teased, never wanting to let go of him. Solomon was her every fantasy brought to life. Now she just had to convince him to keep her.

Incensed, Solomon's gunmetal gaze darkened and turned molten, hungry as he stared at her. Flutters erupted in her core. Lizzie was ready for anything he wanted to do to her. He murmured, a fierce, seductive smile hovering on his lips, "No, I'm going to blister this pretty ass of yours," his hands squeezed the globes and leaned in close to whisper in her ear, "until you can't sit without thinking about the ways in which you handled this incorrectly. And to ensure that you never carry out shenanigans like this again."

Unease rippled through her and she said, "But, I—"

"Too late for regrets. You enticed a Dom, mia bella, and lied," he explained, apparently impassive to her plea.

"I didn't lie, I omitted."

"The intent was the same: to deceive," he said, carrying her in his arms over to the couch. "And after this, you won't ever lie to me again."

Chapter 8

Solomon's world boiled down to the feisty, stubborn woman in his arms. *A virgin.* How had this gorgeous woman remained untouched for so long? As much as he knew about Lizzie, that little tidbit had escaped even his powers of perception. He wouldn't have been more shocked if she'd pointed a gun at his head and pulled the trigger.

She'd chosen *him.* Fuck, it humbled him. *My Lizzie.* This was new territory, even for him.

Then there was the possessive claim of his dominant nature. The moment he penetrated her, claimed her, broke through that thin membrane and felt her silken heat encase his dick, the first man ever to do so, a part of him had simply said: *mine.* Solomon knew deep down he didn't have a right to her, even if he did crave her with every fiber of his being.

Last night, when he'd walked away from her like the blithering idiot he was, he'd had no idea of the damage he'd wrought. She'd chosen him to be her first. Why she'd done it—picked him when he didn't deserve it in the slightest—he hadn't a fucking clue. And he would hoard the experience in his recall to withdraw later.

She'd given him a gift, his precious, beautiful Lizzie. He knew that now. And he had tossed it away and hurt her. It shamed him. He, more than anyone, understood her past, how distant her parents were with her—and that fucktard of an ex-fiancé was hardly any better.

Tonight, he wasn't going to worry about the repercussions or recriminations. Those would come later. His claim had been staked on her and he wasn't letting her go just yet. That would come. And perhaps a better man would end it now, send her on her way, and never touch her again…

But Solomon wasn't a good man—at least, not good enough for his Lizzie, nor would he ever be. If there was anyone who deserved the best life had to offer, it was her. And he would do what was right by her, but not tonight. He was already hell bound, and was a selfish bastard when it came down to it. They'd have to separate him from her with dynamite because for the next eight hours, she belonged to him.

None of those thoughts stalled the fury that rose in his chest, however. The little minx would have given herself to Michael and Dante if Sol had not intervened. Christ, she was untrained and unsullied. She never would have survived a night with those two intact. There was nothing wrong with them, they were damn fine Doms in their own right, but they were demanding and exacting of a submissive. They tended to push a sub's boundaries to the limit. A night with them would have hurt her, changed her, done away with her innocent, vivacious spirit because she would have never understood why they didn't keep her afterward. Those two weren't known for keeping a sub, they tended to prefer variety. And Lizzie was a woman a man kept.

And what was he? Certainly not her white knight. But he was already damned, so if he was bound for hell, at least he would take the memory of this night with him.

Solomon sat down on the couch, sinking into the cushions that had been built with a Dom's comfort in mind. Without much pretense, he arranged Lizzie so that her beautiful butt, bared to him, lay across his thighs. Perfectly formed white mounds, he caressed the supple flesh. Parting them, he stared at her cleft, resisting the urge to plunge his fingers into her succulent pussy. He wanted to bite the mounds of her ass, leave his mark all over her. Make it clear to every fucking Dom on Pleasure Island that she belonged to him.

"What do you think you are doing, Sol? Stop, what gives you the right?" Lizzie bucked against his hold, tension visible in the lines of her lithe back. Her schoolgirl skirt was still bunched around her hips.

"Mia bella, this is why I told you no. You are not built for my world. But this week, you will be forced to submit your will to mine. I'm disciplining you, teaching you that when you lie and act out, there are consequences to those actions. And I have the only right as your Dom this week."

"For the whole week?" she squeaked.

"Mmm-hmm. That's what your actions led to. I will not go back in front of Jared and be made a fool of, nor before the Masters of Underworld, who you were so foolish to throw yourself at this evening. Now hold still."

He laid his left arm across her lower back and spied the traces of blood on her inner thighs. She'd be sore tomorrow, but he'd make it up to her. Lifting his arm, he let his hand fall against her rump. At her undignified screech, he smiled. His Lizzie was the only woman who ever tangled him up and made him question himself.

"Foolish? Are you kidding me?" She reared against his hold but did not have the strength to move him, or escape his hold. "I only did it because you turned me down, you idiot. That's not foolish, it's self-preservation. How about we spank *your* ass and see how you like it?"

His hand fell with another loud crack against her posterior. Her pearlescent skin enflamed.

"Ouch! Sol, cut it out. I mean it," she blustered, and he heard the sob lodged in her voice. He had to stand firm on this. As much as it pained him to cause her distress of any kind, the sooner she understood what a Dominant truly was, the sooner she would understand that this world was not for her. It was the only way he could ensure that when the time came, she was the one who walked away.

Because, selfish bastard that he was, he wasn't certain he had the wherewithal to let her go.

Solomon chastised her, still spanking her bare bottom, walloping her derrière with a few good whacks. She held herself tense against him. This was a lesson. Until she surrendered to his discipline, he would continue. She wanted him? Well, now she had him... for better or worse.

Except her heartrending sobs stirred him, bringing forth the urge to cuddle her close and soothe her. Resolute in his course, he didn't halt—not yet. She still held herself rigid, fighting his dominance and not allowing herself to submit. Solomon had to prove to her that he was the one in charge here; display the full context of what a true Dominant and submissive relationship entailed. She'd played with two Doms this evening who would not have taken kindly to her sass or her fire. Quite the opposite, in fact, they would have broken her with their dominance and demand. At least, they would have tried, anyhow. Knowing Lizzie, she would have gone nuclear and walked away. And that part that he loved most about her, her inherent ability to rebound and still find joy in life, would be forever scarred.

Because of that fear, he peppered her behind, tanning the smooth skin of her hide, the globes pink and blushing from his fervent touch. And still she held herself rigid, fighting his dominance.

"Lizzie, let go, mia bella. Stop trying to top from the bottom, and submit. This is what it means to be in my world. You said you wanted me, now you have me. But it will be on my terms, not yours."

A ragged sob tore from her throat. He blistered her cheeks, watching them redden beneath his hand, branding her as his. Then her entire frame became fluid against him. He felt her submission, her trust in him as she surrendered herself into his care, clear through to his soul. The heady, musky fragrance of her arousal pervaded his nostrils. His cock, the randy, needy bastard it was, strained against her belly.

Solomon would have liked nothing more than to slide inside her wet folds, feel her tight sheath, like heated fucking silk, wrap around him as he unleashed his lust upon her. He had multitudes of fantasies to explore after thirteen years of watching and protecting, craving but never touching. His list would come later, and he planned to tick the items off one at a time.

After the gifts she'd bestowed upon him tonight, her innocence and submission, he needed to show her how her first time should have been. There would be no bondage and no kink. He would make love to his Lizzie—just for tonight, he would be the man she needed, even though she deserved so much more.

Solomon stayed his hand and massaged her fiery globes. Her cries shook her tiny frame and he gathered her close. More precious than any jewels, his Lizzie was the most beautiful, giving woman of his acquaintance. His desire to protect her settled over him and he offered her his strength as she laid her head against his chest. Possessiveness descended over him while she clung so sweetly, so trustingly and innocently to him. He did what he had yearned to do with her for years, and cradled her slight form. Sobs wracked her body. He laid his head against her crown, crooning to her, soothing her with his touch.

"Mia bella, I'm here. Let it all out."

She burrowed deeper against his chest, her nails gouged his flesh, and a part of himself that he'd always held back with her slid into place. He was no one's white knight, but he would guard her, be her constant protector, even after their week together was done. He'd stand sentinel and watch over her, forever.

"Lizzie, I've got you."

He rocked her, held her as the storm raged through her. Her body softened as her sobs turned to hiccups and her tears began to dry.

"I'm sorry, Sol. I didn't mean to trap you. I've just been so lost, and I thought—"

"I know, Lizzie. Tell me why you were still a virgin, why your fiancé never took you to his bed. I can't seem to wrap my head around that one," he admitted. In the thirteen years they'd been friends, he had never once guessed.

"You mean the fact that I was the oldest virgin in the world?" she murmured against his chest, some of her spunky attitude returning.

He chuckled against her hair. "Yes. I'm just trying to understand." And to fully understand the gift she'd given him, and that she had chosen him. In all his life, he'd never received a more precious offering.

"You and me both. Oh, Sol, it was so silly, and I was an inept fool. My parents had such a tight rein on me, even in college, that I was too busy for dating. It's not that I didn't want to, but any time I stepped a toe out of line, they made their displeasure known. You know that. How many times did you see me upset at Julliard? They controlled every aspect of my life. And I wanted to please them. I was desperate for whatever scraps of affection they gave me. When I stayed within the boundaries they set, achieved the goals they set for me, was the only time they ever seemed to like me. So I played it safe and didn't date. I know I grew up with other advantages. I thought it was just one little sacrifice, and my success did make them happy. But there was no warmth from them. Regardless of the fact that my parents could afford to pay my tuition to all the best schools, and hired the best tutors for me growing up. Anyhow, it was easier, safer, to toe their line."

"And you wanted them to love you," he murmured. Some of this, he'd known. He'd met her parents years ago. Both were cold fish. It made him wonder at times how Lizzie had been conceived. For all their warmth, he would have guessed in a laboratory.

"Yes. They never really have, you know. My worth was measured in the prestige I could bring them as a child prodigy. It was never about me, rather a reflection of them. It's taken me years to understand that my upbringing wasn't normal. Anyway, once I'd graduated from Julliard and began performing with the London Symphony Orchestra, my parents introduced me to Edward. They made it known what they expected of me. They wanted the marriage. Me, I was rather indifferent to it and to him, but I was still toeing their line."

"But that doesn't explain why he never took you to his bed, mia bella. If you had been mine, there wouldn't have been a night I'd have gone without you."

He noticed the smile hovering over her lips and she cleared her throat. "Yes, well. He was the one who proposed we wait until we were married. As I didn't much care for him, and was more concerned with my career, I thought nothing of it. Then, every time we went to set a date for the wedding, something came up for him, and we delayed it for another year. And you know, deep down, I was relieved. Neither of us wanted to marry the other. I had convinced myself at the time that I loved him. But truth be told, I didn't even like him. And then I discovered him with Marcella—in my bed and apartment, mind you—and it all just fell apart.

"And I did what I did yesterday because I've spent my whole life with people who didn't care about me, including my parents. But you've always been my best friend and have always shown me more care, even when we are sniping at one another, than those who were supposed to love me. Which is why, out of anyone, I wanted to be with you." She looked at him then, his beautiful Lizzie, an air of fragile vulnerability around her. Like she expected him to crush her heart into dust.

"And then I said no. Mia bella, if I'd known…" He sighed. He likely would have put her on the first ferry off the island and gotten her as far away from the temptation she presented as possible. But now, he couldn't leave her this way: thinking, he could tell, that she was in some way unlovable. His Lizzie had always been his untouchable dream. She was too pure and good, and all the things a man would want, if he were the type of man she needed.

"Yes?" she asked with a whisper that he felt along his spine.

He infused the smirk that spread across his lips with every drop of carnal hunger he had for her. Covering his epic blunder, he focused on her mouth and the steady rise and fall of her chest, the way her nipples beaded beneath his stare, and said, "It doesn't matter now. What matters is how your first time should have been. And I plan to rectify that mistake, right now."

"Oh," she said. Her eyes widened and her pupils dilated.

With her body cradled in his arms, he rose from the couch. Her slight weight reminded him how delicate she was as he strode over to his bed. This time, Solomon planned to take his time, explore her body, show her how good lovemaking could be, and perhaps, in some small way, give her back the gift she'd so willing given him. She'd chosen him.

And for tonight, he would love her the way she deserved.

Chapter 9

Lizzie's stomach performed somersaults and tumbling acrobatics as Sol gently laid her down upon his bed. She stared at him, wordlessly drinking in his handsome appearance. He finally shucked his black leather pants and helped her out of her skirt. The effect on her hormones was razor sharp and she moaned in the back of her throat. Her arousal and need for him caused tremors to riddle her core. Lizzie had never thought a man could be beautiful, but Solomon —tall, sleek, with his testosterone alpha Domness emanating from his being as he stood next to the bed, nude, his erection proudly jutting out between his hips—was all that and more. Her big, beautiful Italian man took her breath away.

He had wide, firm shoulders and a broad chest, the muscles sleek and sinewy. For a man so large, he moved with a grace and ease that was uncommon. A smattering of dark hair covered his pectorals and tapered into a narrow line that neatly bisected down over his abdominals. He'd always been an active man but seeing the defined six-pack, the way the muscles seemed to stretch and bunch as he moved, gave Lizzie the distinct urge to trace her tongue over them. The man was always in control.

His hips were lean, and led to powerful thighs that were more suited to playing on a soccer field than the piano. But it was the firm ridge of his broad, long shaft that fascinated her the most. He was simply huge there. Just like he was everywhere else, but seeing the proof protruding from his pelvis as he left her on the bed and headed into the bathroom, only to return with a warm washcloth, made an ache and slow burn start in her core.

His long fingers parted her legs. Then he drew the cloth over her thighs and her most intimate flesh. She bit her bottom lip at the unexpected pleasure.

After he had tossed the damp cloth into a nearby hamper, he climbed up and joined her on his bed. The mattress dipped beneath his weight. He stretched out beside her, his large body dwarfing hers. His hand cupped her cheek with a tenderness that brought moisture to her eyes. His large thumb caressed her upper lip, the pad whispering against her flesh, electrifying her nerve endings. Except it was his eyes, near black and scorching with desire for her, which stole her breath. Air clogged in her lungs. She trembled beneath him.

Solomon wanted her. Lizzie couldn't seem to believe it or wrap her brain around that tidbit, nor stop the joy from spreading over her at the thought. After all this time, he wasn't turning her away. She reached for him, yearning to touch him, to explore the hard planes and firm muscles that had been denied her for so long. But he caught her hands with one of his larger ones and pinned them above her head.

When she opened her mouth to protest, he brushed his lips over hers and murmured, the command inherent in his tone, "Just let me love you. Keep your hands above your head and give yourself over into my care tonight."

He lifted his head slightly, his gaze boring into hers, and she sighed. She wondered what he would find in her eyes. Would he see how much she yearned for him? How she'd walked around for years knowing that no man had ever made her feel quite like he did? How, if truth be told, she'd wanted him since the day they'd first met thirteen years ago? She remembered their initial meeting like it had happened yesterday. She had cherished it, because it was the day he'd brought her to life. Until that moment, all she'd ever done was exist. His midnight hair had been longer then, brushing his wide shoulders. He'd smiled down at her, his hands holding her steady after she'd nearly plowed him over on her way to class, and there'd been no looking back. Her heart had fallen for him then and there.

And she'd never truly gotten it back.

"Lizzie," he said, with a guttural growl which rumbled in his chest and vibrated through her. Solomon claimed her lips, covered her mouth with his and demanded a response from her. Lizzie had been kissed loads of times by her fiancé, she'd pushed for those since she wasn't getting any nookie. But not one had ever turned her inside out, carved its initials on her soul, and caused flames to lick over her body and send her up in smoke.

She returned his kiss, no longer hesitating to brush her tongue against his but succumbing to the passion as it roiled between them. He re-forged her. Molded her with his lips. Dominance poured from him as he commanded a response from her mouth, from her body, and she exulted in the sensations. She existed because he made it so. She throbbed in seductive agony because he knew precisely how to elicit a response from her.

Solomon released her hands, his own caressing her so that she moaned into his mouth. Lizzie dug her fingers into the mattress, complying with his request to keep her hands above her head. She grabbed at the pillows, clenching their softness in her fists. But it was difficult when she ached to touch him, feel how the muscles in his back moved as he shifted over her.

Then his mouth lifted and she couldn't stop her whimper. She wanted him to keep kissing her. He flashed her a sensual grin and began a carnal exploration of her physique. He started with his hands, like he was committing her figure to memory as he traced the gentle swell of her breasts, learning their shape and size. Her nipples puckered into stiff points as the pads of his thumbs scraped over them. He teased the heart-shaped beauty mark beneath her right mound.

His thumb circled and flicked over her nipple. Pleasure speared from her chest to her core and she moaned in the back of her throat. Whereas before it had been a heated rush to the finish line, this time, Solomon meandered and discovered, taking his time, studying her face to see what elicited a heady response, and what made her wail in an agony of need.

When his fingers lightly caressed her mound, one finger grazing teasingly through her folds, Lizzie understood that what he had planned was not going to be fast or easy, but exquisite torture. She'd likely expire from the sheer volume of pleasure. Her legs parted wider of their own accord, granting him access.

His fingers teased her clit, rubbing against the swelling nub and ripping a moan from deep within her chest. Through it all, his gaze stayed on hers, paying attention to each minute gasp and moan. Her lids became heavy as her need grew. She needed—*oh, my*—him. Her breath expelled in short pants. Her nipples stabbed toward the ceiling as he stroked her to orgasm and she soared as her body imploded.

"Sol," she wailed.

Lizzie vibrated within the circle of his arms as he wrung every drop of ecstasy from her. And that was just with his fingers. He played her body as expertly as he did a concerto.

She raised her arms, reaching for him, but he stilled her. He nipped her bottom lip and murmured, "Just keep your hands at your sides and let me love you, Lizzie."

Then his mouth—*holy moly*—initiated a trail of torture. She'd barely returned to planet earth after that first climax and he was already driving her body back up another intoxicating precipice. He rained hungry, open-mouthed kisses along her shoulders and the hollow of her neck. His name became a litany on her lips as he progressed over her skin, swiping his tongue over a rigid peak of her nipple before his mouth eagerly descended over it. He lavished her breasts with his tongue and teeth, his lips brushing against the sensitive underside. Solomon paid particular attention to the mole beneath her right boob.

She gripped the sheets, keening at every new sensation as his mouth traveled south. He sucked so firmly against her skin in places that he left marks. His marks. His teeth nipped and bit at her flesh. And she was catapulted out of the stratosphere when his teeth grazed her clitoris. He growled against her sex, sliding his tongue through the drenched heat of her labia folds.

Then Solomon plunged his tongue inside her quivering channel. Lizzie arched her back, rising up off the sheets at the shocking intensity of pleasure as it whipped through her body. With his big, firm hands, he gripped her hips, making her a prisoner as he feasted on her pussy. Wrenching moans and throaty whimpers from her while his mouth devoured her engorged nub. His tongue—*sweet merciful heavens*, did he have a talented tongue. The man knew just how to drive her body to the edge and hold it there as he lashed her clit with fast flicks, then drew the pleasure out as he inserted his tongue, thrusting and plunging deep, only to withdraw and begin the torture all over again.

Lizzie was climbing a sheer cliff, ascending the heights of pleasure. Need clawed through her so that she was a writhing, undulating mass of desire—and his to command.

"Sol," she wailed, her back arching further as he took her up and over the edge. Her body was his personal playground. She whimpered as her tremors subsided. Lizzie needed to feel him inside her, wanted him to fill her, connect with her on the deepest level. She yearned for the sensation of his heavier weight on top of her, but he didn't cease his erotic endeavors.

Again, she had barely finished shuddering from one mind-blowing climax before Solomon was there, hurtling her body up the next, this one more blinding than the last. His fingers joined the fray and worked in tandem. His uber-talented mouth consumed her clit, sucking the turgid flesh into his mouth, while his fingers penetrated and thrust inside her pussy. Lizzie fought for purchase, attempting to keep a toehold on reality.

Solomon lifted his face. His chin glistened with her dew, lust shrouded his dark gaze, all while his fingers pumped in a methodical, earth shattering rhythm, not stopping the delicious pleasure but adding to it. In a deep bedroom voice that made her toes curl, he ordered, "Just let go, mia bella. I'll catch you when you fall."

Then his hungry mouth descended once more and Lizzie couldn't stop her orgasm from rendering her brainless any more than she could stop her heart from loving Sol. While knowing that should terrify her, it didn't. She'd loved him since the first day they had met. And that love had only deepened with time. It was partly the reason why when her engagement had gone belly up—she'd not been that terribly upset and had been relieved, more than anything.

Solomon added a third digit, taking her body up again and again.

"Please, Sol, please," she begged, so mindless with need she could see only him.

He glanced up at her from between her thighs with such desire, her breath shuddered out of her lungs. She knew he had commanded that she keep her arms at her sides but she needed to touch him, beckoning him into her embrace.

Solomon rose over her, settling his weight between her spread thighs. At the feel of his swollen, erect cock as he rubbed the crest through her weeping folds, she moaned. "Sol, please."

Gripping his cock, he positioned his rock hard shaft at her entrance. Their gazes clashed and held. Their breaths mingled. Then, with exquisite care, he thrust with a roll of his hips. Her eyes widened as he penetrated her, pushing deep until his sack pressed against her rear.

This was what heaven felt like. Here, in his arms, his cock embedded inside her. It was a place she never wanted to leave. He held still, allowing her body to adjust to his length and girth. His weight pressed her into the mattress. As her body altered to accommodate his, need began to override everything. She wriggled her hips, wanting him to move, create some friction… if he would just move already.

Solomon flashed her a sexy grin, knowing full well that he was driving her crazy. Then he gripped both her hands, pinning them on either side of her shoulders, and threaded his fingers through hers as he withdrew until only the tip remained before thrusting forward until he hit the lip of her womb. She groaned at the exquisite pleasure. Instinct borne of need and pulse-pounding desire won as her hips undulated beneath him. Solomon's thrusts made stars erupt and she plunged further into the abyss of ecstasy. She was captivated by his spell as he filled her near to bursting… and then would retreat.

He rolled his hips, plunging deeper, making himself a part of her. She poured her feelings for him into her eyes, holding nothing back.

"Lizzie," Sol cried on a ragged breath and slanted his mouth over hers. He released her hands, pulling her tighter against him, claiming her lips. Her body became fused with his as he thrust. She was finally able to touch him. Gripping his sweat-slicked back, her hands dug into his muscles, slid to his lower back and held on, attempting to tug him even deeper.

It had become a raw, uninhibited fight to the finish line—one that she never wanted to end. He made love to her, and parts of herself mended. He made her whole, filled the gaps of her aching heart and repaired her soul. The way he hoarsely whispered her name as he drank her startled cries… The orgasm originated from within the deepest recesses of her core, an erupting geyser that rattled her foundation. She clung to him as she came apart.

"Sol," she wailed as tears fell from her eyes.

Then he strained, vibrating against her as he spurted, his cock jolting in her clasping folds. Tossing his head back, he bellowed his completion, his hips still thrusting, drawing out the pleasure until the last vestiges had been wrung from their bodies.

Spent, he collapsed against her, burying his face in the hollow of her neck. His breathing was shallow, puffing out against her skin as their heartrates returned to normal. Lizzie clutched him, keeping him a prisoner within her arms. She never wanted to let him go.

Then he shifted up onto his elbows and gazed down at her, his eyes molten. He tenderly cupped her face, and her heart trembled. Maybe wishes really did come true. Solomon kissed her, lovingly poured himself into the embrace, stalling the words her heart longed for her to finally say.

But it was all right as he rolled from her body, then tucked her close against him, spooning her from behind. With a yawn, her eyes slid shut. There'd be plenty of time for that later.

Chapter 10

Lizzie stretched, deliciously sore, but filled with a deep-seated contentment the likes of which she'd never experienced before. Blinking at the sunshine streaming in through the balcony windows, she searched for Solomon.

When she didn't spy him in the room, she rose, clutching the sheets to her chest. Then she heard the water running in the bathroom. Why didn't he wake her? Worrying her bottom lip, she slid from the bed. After the night they'd had, surely he wouldn't push her away, would he?

She wished she was more experienced and knew what to expect. But her heart was involved, it had been involved from the beginning. Intimacy was new territory, and she had no idea what he expected from her.

She walked silently into the bathroom, the door quiet as she pushed it open. Solomon stood beneath the hot spray. His gloriously nude form stirred her loins. He had awakened the carnal creature that had been asleep inside her and now that it was aware, arousal hummed in her veins at the mere sight of him.

Going on instinct, she silently opened the shower door and joined him. Steam rose from the scalding hot water. He still hadn't heard her yet. She slipped her arms around his waist, pressing her length against his back.

Solomon didn't jerk in surprise, only glanced over his shoulder at her and said, "I thought you were still in bed. You didn't need to get up yet. It was a long night."

She shrugged against him, holding him close, and replied, "I missed you."

A pained look lanced across his features and he said, "Lizzie."

A code red warning blared inside her brain. Without thinking about the consequences, she pressed her lips against his back. She tried copying the way he'd done the open-mouthed ones on her last night and added her tongue, tasting his skin. Her hands slid down from his waist and wrapped around his cock.

Solomon hissed, "Lizzie."

But he didn't stop her. She nipped at his back muscles while her hands caressed his shaft. Using the moisture from the shower, she stroked his length with one hand while the other fondled his sack. Solomon dropped his head down and braced his hands on the tile wall, giving her full permission to explore his body.

Lizzie learned his body by touch alone. Plastering herself against his back, she stroked his cock. She rubbed his crown, caressing the ridge with her fingers, tracing the veins, loving the soft skin. Laying her cheek against his strong back, she closed her eyes, absorbing every minute shift of his muscles.

She discovered which caresses made Solomon hiss, which made him tremble, and which ones made his hips buck wildly. Lizzie thought she'd been aroused before. But last night had apparently just been the tip of the freaking iceberg. Just like he had done with her body the night before, she took him to the edge—or as near it as she could sense—then backed off, slowing her strokes. Over and over, she gauged his response, enjoying the feel of the big bad Dom at her mercy.

At least, until he'd had enough of her teasing. His hand fisted around hers on his cock, increasing the tempo of the caress. Meanwhile, his hips thrust in rapid succession, his moans filling the steamy shower. Then he jerked, his cock swelled, and he roared her name.

A stream of cum spewed forth and splattered against the shower wall. She didn't release him until his own hand slackened. But then he was turning and propelling her up against the wall. His lips claimed hers in a heated exchange. She never knew it could be like this. Fun and sexy, exciting and thrilling. And she was glad it was Solomon she got to experience it with.

He tugged her over to the padded bench and sat, then yanked her onto his lap. How was the man still hard? He arranged her body so that her back was now flush against his chest. As though they had exchanged places. He spread her thighs wide so that her legs rested on the outside of each of his.

And then he was fitting his shaft at her entrance and feeding it into her greedy pussy. She gasped as pleasure stole all rational thought. He hugged her close as he lazily fucked her. His left hand descended to her sex, rubbing her clit and adding to the delicious stimulation. Her head fell back against his chest.

His right hand teased her nipples, cupped her breasts. She mewled and writhed, wishing he would pick up the pace a bit. Just a bit more friction and she would come. Likely more than once, the way he did things. She blew out a frustrated breath that turned into a loud moan.

"Sol, please," she begged, all pride completely forgotten.

The hand on her breast moved up to her chin. He shifted her face to the side and his mouth slanted over hers, swallowing her cries. There was no hurry in him. She was completely and utterly at his mercy as he pumped his shaft in lazy strokes. His fingers thrummed over her clitoris. Pleasure simmered and boiled, but he kept her body on this delicious, carnal ledge, not allowing her release but never letting her come down either.

It was the most erotic moment of her life.

They were as intimately connected as two people could be but she wanted more. Her hand slid around his neck and held his mouth over hers. Or at least gave her the illusion she controlled him in that. She was fully aware that if Solomon didn't want her to touch him, he would have stopped her. But since he didn't, she kissed him with all the pent-up desire and frustration flowing in her body. Every single ounce of need he created in her, she gave back to him with her lips.

It elicited the same reaction dropping a match on nitroglycerin would have. Still connected, his erection furrowing deep within her, he shifted their bodies until they were kneeling on the bench. Her front was pressed against the shower glass, Solomon's fingers were digging into her hips, and he pounded inside her clenching heat. Her cheek lay against the glass, her palms flat as she whimpered at the brutal fucking.

It was so good. She couldn't move, couldn't do anything as he jackhammered his cock inside her quaking channel. But she loved every minute of it.

She whimpered, she wailed, and when the tidal wave of her climax finally hit, it decimated her composure. She shattered as she shook and vibrated, dimly aware of Solomon as he trumpeted his release. Hot liquid filled her sheath, causing a secondary series of aftershocks.

When Solomon withdrew, she slid bonelessly down to the bench. He cared for her then. Washing her body and cleaning between her thighs before he shut the water off. He enveloped her in a thick fluffy towel and carried her back into the bedroom.

Instead of putting her into bed, he strode out onto the balcony and settled into a chair with her still in his lap. She instinctively curled up against him. Her eyelids heavy, she drifted, knowing she was safe and protected with him.

Chapter 11

Solomon knew he was perilously close to the point of no return where Lizzie was concerned. All day long, throughout their performances, he guarded her, shielded her from other Doms. The fact that he wanted to blind any man who so much as looked at her with something more than respect, let him know he was walking a fine line.

Was this how his dad had felt before he'd murdered his mother's lover? This overwhelming desire to keep his woman from the rest of the world?

It was undeniable: Lizzie was his in the deepest way possible. But as he gazed out across the inky blackness of the ocean, rolling like a great beast while he stood on his balcony as Lizzie let room service in with their dinner, he knew he couldn't allow this thing between them to continue past tonight.

His open dress shirt fluttered in the breeze. It was going to hurt her. He knew that. Just thinking about the looks she'd tossed his way today, his heart squeezed. He didn't want to let her go. Christ, he loved her, but he couldn't risk the seed of his father inside him destroying her.

There was a reason why he was a Dom. It was a way for him

to keep his emotions in check, erect a barrier between himself and whatever woman he was fucking. He'd watched how passionately his father had loved his mother. And he'd also been watching on the day his father had returned home to find his mother in bed with another man.

The passion his father had always held had turned into a potent rage that didn't stop until he'd beaten the other man to death. In front of Solomon and his mum. Sol could still hear his mother's screams. He remembered the Garda as they'd stormed into their home and dragged his father off to prison. His mum had sent him to live with his aunt in Manhattan then. He'd been sixteen. His dad had died in prison, in a fight with another prisoner, and Sol's relationship with his mother had never recovered.

Ever since that fateful night, he had lived with the murderous ghost of his father.

His dad had always told Sol how alike they were in temperament. Which was why he would give himself and Lizzie tonight before ending it. He would show her a small slice of the lifestyle, give himself this chance to love her with everything he was, because once the sun crested the horizon, it would be done between them.

He was a right bloody bastard and he knew it. A better man would send her on her way tonight. But he wanted this night—needed it—before he sent her off to love another man. For she would; his Lizzie was a passionate, loving woman who deserved the best a man had to offer, and Sol knew it wasn't him. She deserved to be protected and cherished. Even when that meant protecting her from himself.

When dawn came, he wouldn't touch her again. No matter how much it killed him.

Her arms slid around him from behind and he closed his eyes at the pleasure.

"Dinner's here. Why don't you come inside?" she said, her hands teasing the waistband of his slacks.

He was painfully erect in his pants, then again, that seemed to be the case whenever Lizzie was near him.

"Is there something else you need?" he teased, as he compartmentalized the coming pain and separation. A little trick he'd learned when his life had fallen apart as a teen.

"You. Always you," she said, making his heart squeeze, and then she bit his back.

"Ow. What the hell was that for?" Solomon asked, shifting in her arms and scowling down at her.

"I just felt like it. You seemed to have unleashed this wanton, and she wants to do all sorts of crazy things to you." She gave him a sly, seductive grin.

"Is that right? What things?" he purred, pulling her close and making sure she understood exactly what her nearness did to him.

Her breath hitched and her eyes widened, but then she said, "Come eat dinner with me and then I will show you, but not until then…"

The little termagant.

"Who the hell is the Dom here?" he asked, bemused at her antics. He might have to give her another lesson in discipline tonight.

She shrugged and gave him a gamine grin. "Oh, it's definitely you, but I can't help it if I have a hard time resisting you. That's all you."

Christ, he didn't know if one night would be enough. "Lizzie…" He sighed and bent his head down to hers, covering her mouth with his. He kissed her until she became pliant against him. Only then did he raise his head.

"That's playing dirty pool," she said, raising a golden eyebrow.

"It is, but one does what one must. Now…" He bent and hoisted her over his shoulder.

She screeched, "Sol, put me down, you idiot."

"Idiot, huh?" He turned his face and bit her hip, hard, just as his arm banded about her thighs and his free hand smacked her rump. She squealed and he chuckled darkly. Oh hell yeah, he was introducing her into the lifestyle tonight. She was ripe for it.

As he walked them back into his room, to the dining table with their meal, Lizzie's hand smacked across his butt check. He stilled, more shocked than anything that she would do that to him. When it happened a second time, he didn't know whether to be pissed off or amused. He shifted her in his arms and set her down on her feet.

"What the hell was that, Lizzie? You spanked a Dom. That's not how this works."

"I couldn't breathe, you big dolt. Your shoulder was digging into my diaphragm and I didn't know how to get your attention. Besides, it was just two little love taps. I'm sure a big bad Dom like you can handle it."

"Oh, I'll handle it all right—and pull you across my knees. See if I don't."

"Fine, go ahead. But can we eat first? I'm starved."

Solomon knew he should discipline her, knew that most Doms wouldn't hesitate to punish her, but he didn't want to ruin the night. So he chose laughter instead, chuckling at his Lizzie's antics as he had on so many occasions when they'd been just friends.

He would miss this, for surely she would hate him come morning.

"Ah, Lizzie, you never fail to entertain me. Let's eat quick, before you do something I really will have to punish you for."

He ushered her into her chair and poured her a glass of her favorite cabernet. He opened the bottle of Guinness for himself and sat across from her at the square dining table. They'd ordered steaks and salads. Then there was the cook's mouthwatering pumpernickel bread, hot and fresh from the oven, with whipped butter.

As they dug in, Lizzie asked, "So I've wondered, what is it about the lifestyle that always attracted you? I know we never really talked about it all these years, even though I knew when we were at Julliard—"

Taken aback, he asked, "You did? I didn't parade my preferences around. At least, not until after I graduated and had a job."

After a sip of wine, she shrugged and said, "People talk. And you forget how much we hung out in college. There aren't many college guys with a closet full of leather pants."

"You went through my things, Lizzie, I'm surprised." He wondered what else she knew that he'd kept hidden. Did she know about his dad too? He'd never talked about him, not with anyone.

"Not intentionally. Remember the night of the after party, where I got sick?"

"You mean where you were tossing back shots of whisky like a pro, and ended up praying to the porcelain god for the remainder of the night? Yes. If I recall, I was the one who held your hair back."

She nodded. "And took care of me during my first hangover. Well, when you left your room to get us breakfast that morning, after I took a shower, I was looking for a shirt to wear that wasn't covered in vomit, and accidentally happened across your stash of fetish wear."

"I see. And why did you never bring it up with me?" he asked, curious. They'd talked about everything else.

"I didn't know how you felt about it at the time, and didn't want to embarrass you or make you think I was snooping. I figured, since we were friends, when you were ready to tell me, you would."

Leave it to Lizzie to always give a person the benefit of the doubt. She was too good for her own good, dammit. Always choosing to see the best in people. And he was touched that she had, in her way, protected his secret before he'd made it known and stopped trying to hide it. "What do I like about it? I need the control, Lizzie. I enjoy feeling a woman submit her will to mine. It's a power exchange that starts before it even enters the bedroom."

"Oh yeah, like what?" She tilted her head to the side, studying him, absorbing his words.

"In a true Dominant and submissive relationship, respect and trust are mutual, going both ways. Typically, a Dominant cares for his submissive, in a manner the two have agreed upon, usually taking on a submissive's cares and worries, freeing her up to submit fully to her Dom. A Dom and a sub have diverse parts in the dynamic, but they are both equally important. They are two halves of a larger whole, stronger because the other is there. And, honestly, I need to be in control. I always have."

"And how does a submissive know they are pleasing a Dom?" she asked.

Taking a final sip of his beer, he set the empty bottle on the table. He could see where this was going. And he couldn't go there and give her hope that what they had was of the lasting variety.

Instead of reassuring her, as a good Dom would, he kidded, "Whether or not he's got her over his knee, panties around her knees, and peppering her ass with a firm spanking."

She colored prettily. He rose from his chair, enjoying the way her gaze caressed him. He plucked her from her seat, carting her over to the bed. He set her on the edge and ordered, "Strip."

He left her there, sliding his dress shirt off as he headed around the side to the armoire. He wouldn't take her pretty rosette tonight. As much as he wanted it, he feared that if he claimed her there, he would never let go. But that didn't mean he couldn't push her boundaries and see whether anal was even in the cards for Lizzie. Why it mattered to him, he hadn't a fucking clue. Perhaps to torture himself further.

With the armoire doors open, he selected a slim, beaded, vibrating butt plug. Considering she'd never had sex before him, he had no doubt her ass was virgin territory too, and didn't want to try anything too large for her first anal experience. He grabbed a tube of lubricant, then pulled out a pair of Velcro restraints with a bit of a lead on each one.

Solomon placed his goodies on the nightstand, then stripped the comforter and top sheet down to near the foot of the bed. He picked up the large, black, wedge pillow leaning against the armoire and set it in the middle of the mattress. Then he attached the restraints to the two posts on the headboard, and laid the plug and lube beside the wedge before he finally turned back to one very naked Lizzie.

Her body was lean and taut, it never failed to arouse him. She was so proud, and he burned for her.

"Don't you make a picture. Now, for the rest of tonight, you will address me as Sir or Master. Understood?" He wondered if she would balk at this. A part of him—the part that knew morning would be here before he was ready—wanted her to; it would make the separation easier.

"Yes, Sir. I understand," she murmured prettily.

Aw, fuck! At hearing her say those words, pleasure cascaded through him.

"All right, I want you up in bed, positioned over the wedge, with your ass facing the footboard."

"Um, Sir, could I, um—" She blushed furiously, and glanced away. Lizzie was rarely shy.

Intrigued, he approached, cupped her chin, and lifted her gaze to his. "Finish what you were going to ask me."

"I wondered if we could do one of the things on my list first. I will do whatever you want me to do, but I really want to…"

"What?"

"Taste you, Sir, in my mouth. I want your cock in my mouth," she said, a rosy-hued blush coloring her cheeks.

He sucked in a ragged breath. She was going to kill him. And he couldn't think of anything he wanted more in that moment. He nodded. "Proceed."

Her eyes glazed with need and she licked her lips, sinking to her knees before him. He glanced down and watched as she undid the button and zipper of his slacks, then slid them off his hips and down his legs. He was hard enough—his boxers were tented—and her gaze was studiously on his crotch.

He clenched his hands into fists, wanting to give her a chance to explore before he reeled her in and directed her movements. She torturously unveiled his cock, which seemed to salute her for her forthcoming endeavor as she shoved his boxers down to his feet. He helped her, stepping out of both so that he was standing naked before her.

Her fingers slid around his dick and he hissed at the exquisite pleasure. Holding him steady, she leaned forward, then her pretty pink tongue darted out and swiped over his crown, lapping at the tiny bead of pre-cum. He gritted his teeth. Her unschooled movements tested his willpower when she closed her mouth around the head, looking up at him through her thick, inky lashes. Then she sucked his length down, swallowing his cock into the hot chamber of her mouth.

Christ, it felt like heaven. Unable to hold back, Solomon groaned as she stroked him, moving her mouth up and down his dick. His eyes damn near rolled back in his head. She flicked her tongue along the vein underneath, drew it up the length of his cock, and then swished it teasingly around the head.

Fuck, where had she learned that? He was shaking, trembling as she gave him head.

Lizzie's eyes slid shut, the pleasure obvious on her face as she began to suck him in earnest. Sol fucking lost it, watching her head bob up and down over his cock, her mouth like a fucking firebrand, drawing him deep. She hollowed her cheeks and took him deeper. Her chest heaved as she breathed. Her nipples beaded and he could smell her arousal, the musky fragrance that was all Lizzie.

Unable to stand it anymore, he gripped her head between his hands, holding her steady as he thrust unabashed into her mouth. She moaned around his dick. The sound nearly brought him to his knees. She slid her hands around to his ass and dug her nails in, enjoying the experience as much as he. It felt like she was trying to inhale him, taste every part of him. She was a fucking natural, at all of it.

But deep down, he'd always known she would be.

Lightning streaked down his spine. His balls drew up and tightened. His cock lengthened, swelling inside her pretty mouth. Molten lava spurted up from his sack and his seed exploded into her mouth as he pumped his hips, growling his release. She lapped up his cum, drinking him down.

When she had finished, she sat back on her haunches, her breath coming in short, sharp pants. He hoisted her into his arms and crushed his mouth over his. His taste on her lips fueled his hunger for her.

When she leaned against him, surrendering to his kiss, he lifted his head. Her pupils were large and her eyes glazed with passion. No more waiting.

He maneuvered her over to the bed and then explained, "I'm going to restrain just your hands this time, Lizzie. If something hurts or is uncomfortable, I want you to use the safeword, red, understood?"

"Yes, Sir."

"Good. Now, get your cute butt situated over the wedge."

Lizzie followed his orders as he asked. Her killer body, once she had settled over the wedge, made him wish for things that would never be. Ignoring his heartache, he gently fastened her wrists into the Velcro restraints.

"Very good. I'm proud of you. These don't feel too tight, do they?"

"No, Sir," she said breathlessly, arousal lacing her voice.

"Good. I plan to introduce you a wee bit to anal," he elucidated.

When she gasped, he explained further. "Just a small vibrating plug, Lizzie. The goal here is pleasure, not pain. And it's small enough to see if you enjoy anal at all. If so, there are ways to train your cute little rosette to accept a man's cock. If not, well, then you know."

"Whatever you want, Sir," she said. And that was what he was afraid of: Lizzie was so giving, truly the perfect slate for a submissive. She always wanted to please and would likely be willing and eager to try anything he might suggest.

"For tonight, I just want you to enjoy. So relax, and if something is not to your liking, use the safeword I gave you."

He climbed into bed and crouched behind her upturned ass. Solomon had to take a few deep breaths when he spied the dew slicked over her pussy. He'd never known a woman so ready for his touch. If he were different, and didn't carry the stain of his father... ah, *fuck it*, he couldn't dwell on what he couldn't change.

Solomon positioned her thighs, spreading them to accommodate his girth.

Unable to help himself, he slid his fingers through her crease and heard her gasp. Driven by the need to please her so that she would remember this night, he bent down and ate her juicy cunt. He didn't do it the gentle way of the previous night. No, he stormed her defenses and had her writhing and screaming his name, his face buried between her thighs as she came.

She tasted so fucking sweet. He could eat her plump pussy all fucking night long. He rose, drawing some moisture from her cunt and adding lube to his fingers. Then he pressed his index finger against the puckered hole of her rosette. He heard her indrawn breath and ordered, "Deep breaths, relax for me, Lizzie. I promise you will love it."

She trusted him so much, the tension in her form just fell

away. And it caused his finger to slide further inside. She was tight, but felt like electrified silk. He wished he would be the one to take her here, but that was for another man.

He worked his finger inside her back channel until it was gliding smoothly in and out before he added a second digit. By the time he had the two thrusting in and out with ease, Lizzie was moaning and attempting to tilt her hips up for more. Oh yeah, his Lizzie loved it. Just like he knew she would.

He withdrew his fingers and picked up the small beaded plug. After coating it with more lube, he inserted it into her ass, gently pushing past the resistant tissues until it was fully embedded. Then, because he wanted her to come many times tonight, he flipped the switch on the motor to the highest vibration.

At her indrawn breath, he chuckled.

Then he gripped his cock, rubbing the crown through her dripping folds. She moaned and threshed her head as he teased her. He drew it out, barely sliding the tip inside until she was whimpering and moaning.

"Sir, please," she begged around a gasp.

"Please what?" He wanted her to spell it out for him. It was intoxicating having her mindless with need, awaiting his pleasure.

"Fuck me, Sir, please."

"About fucking time," he growled, and thrust. He seated himself inside her until his balls pressed against her clit, and she groaned.

"Now, hold on, honey, because I plan to fuck you until your goddamn legs fall off."

Her response was a garbled moan. He gritted his teeth as he plunged. He fucked her hard, brutally. Unleashing the animal within. His hands gripped her hips as he plowed inside her sheath. Restrained the way she was, all she could do was take it.

She was the most gorgeous thing he'd ever seen. She reveled in his dominance. The vibrations from the plug made her pussy clench tighter around his shaft as he shuttled his length in and out.

Lizzie came, screaming, her pussy clenching around his cock. But he didn't stop. He changed the angle and leaned forward, propping himself up on his arms as he ground his hips, pummeling her sheath with short, brutal, hard digs.

She keened his name as she came again.

Over and over he plunged. Her eyes were closed, her mouth open on a near constant moan. After her next climax, he withdrew his cock, turned off the plug, and slid it from her rear. He undid her wrist restraints and lifted her off the wedge, giving it a shove off the bed. Then he rolled her onto her back, kneed her thighs apart, and settled his weight between her thighs.

She looked up at him through half-lidded eyes. She bit her bottom lip as he thrust inside and gathered her close. His face was hovering above hers, allowing him to watch every emotion flit across her lovely face. She enveloped him, her legs wrapped around his waist. Her arms were gripped tightly around his neck. And her hips writhed beneath his, meeting his thrusts.

It was his turn to shake. His turn to groan. His turn to quake as she held him close.

When she went over the edge this time, Solomon followed her, promising himself that what was to come was the right thing to do.

He only wished he believed it himself.

Chapter 12

There are days when a girl just shouldn't get out of bed.

When Lizzie woke the following morning, she reached for Solomon. Their night had been epic. Every moment with him held magic for her. A smile hovered over her lips. Last night had been one of the most amazing nights of her life. Her body ached, and her muscles were sore in places she hadn't even realized a body could be sore. But it was the best, most delicious sensation Lizzie had ever encountered.

She felt like her world finally made sense. Solomon had always been the unacknowledged squatter in her heart. Was it any wonder she'd never been able to fully love her ex-fiancé? Hard to do when your heart already belonged to another. It didn't matter that it had taken them thirteen years to get here, it turned out to be worth the wait. He'd always been worth the wait.

When she encountered empty space, Lizzie cracked her eyes open. It was early yet. The sun barely crested the horizon, illuminating the room. Solomon stood at the window, his back to her. He seemed so lonely, in his jeans slung low over his hips and black tee shirt. Still uncomfortable with her own nudity, she wrapped the bed sheet around her body and silently walked to him.

Lizzie had lost time to make up for, and now that she knew precisely what she'd been missing, she didn't want to waste any more time deliberating. They had six hours before they had to be downstairs to perform. And she planned to use every second.

She slid her arms around him, pressed her body up against his back, and whispered, "Good morning."

He stiffened at the contact.

"Sorry, I didn't mean to surprise you. Come back to bed." She lowered her hands. Her fingers sought his sensitive flesh beneath his jeans.

His hands gripped hers before they descended beneath his waistband and stalled her forward progression. "What do you think you're doing?" he bit out caustically.

The sharpness of his voice stilled her. "What's wrong?"

Was he still upset over the whole virgin thing? Once they'd made it past the initial surprise, the last two nights had been wonderful. The last forty-eight hours had been the best of her life, and now he was acting as if it meant nothing.

"Lizzie," he sighed, a distant finality in his voice.

Warning bells began to ring loudly in her ears. This was all wrong. Lizzie didn't understand what was happening. Why was he shutting her out like this? After everything they'd shared, his sudden cold shoulder was ripping her heart to shreds.

"Sol, what's going on? Talk to me, please. I don't understand." She couldn't hide the panic lacing her voice but she didn't care. What was he doing? Was he done with her?

"I know you don't. And I'm sorry, mia bella, but it's never going to happen again," he said, his voice low and flat. All the warmth had somehow been leeched from him overnight. If Lizzie didn't know better, she'd say he'd had his personality snatched by an alien.

She flinched like she'd been struck. "What do you mean?"

But she understood. Deep down, she knew what was happening. Fear unlike anything she'd ever experienced before swam in her breast. Solomon didn't want her anymore. He was tossing her away, like she was yesterday's trash, after everything…

"I will not sleep with you again. Last night was…"

She backed away. Her heart splintered. "Was what, Sol?"

He swiveled from the window then, and faced her. Regret dampened his gunmetal gaze. His countenance was solemn. He said, "A mistake. I never should have touched you. And I won't. Not ever again. You don't belong in my world."

"That's rubbish. We've been in each other's worlds for thirteen years. So you slept with me, and now decide you don't want me in your life?"

"Lizzie, don't be silly. Of course I want you in my life. Just not in that way."

"Was I not good?" She knew she was inexperienced but from the way he'd reacted, she thought he'd been just as blown away by their interactions as she had been. She searched his face, attempting to discern why this was happening.

"Lizzie. I'm sorry if I made you believe the last two nights were anything more than what they were. I never should have touched you. You don't belong in my world or in the lifestyle. You deserve better," he murmured, his face grave, and unforgiving in his stance.

"But you said I'm your sub for the week!" she shouted, scrambling as panic overrode her common sense. She needed to be rational about the cause of his distance. But she was all emotion—there was no logic, only a knee-jerk reaction as terror swamped her.

"And you will be, in name only," he said. "Tonight, and every night, you will come to my room. You can sleep in the bed. I will be on the couch."

"And then you'll what, pretend to like me, pretend to care in front of everyone?" she snapped, fighting back tears. How could he do this to her? Her heart was breaking, shattering like glass into a million jagged pieces.

"It's for the best. And you won't change my mind on this. I'm sorry, Lizzie, truly I am." He said it so quietly, and with such resolve, hot tears splashed over her cheeks. Solomon turned away from her, giving her his back, and shutting her out.

The finality of it broke her. She was done pretending. Lizzie had spent the last seven years pretending to love someone. She knew that what she felt for Solomon was real. But she had no idea how to scale the sudden wall he had erected between them. Straightening her spine, she remarked, "But the last two nights did happen. And I know you felt something. You can lie to yourself all you want, but you forget that I know you. And you can forget about me acting like you're my Dom this week. Either you are, or you aren't. It's not your job to protect me."

He shot her a glance over his shoulder. Anger flashed in his eyes but she ignored it. If he was going to shove her aside after everything, she'd deal. Perhaps not well, but she would.

"As your Dom, it is," he muttered, his face stern and immovable.

"But you said so yourself, you are not mine. Which means I'm not yours. You can't have it both ways. You can't keep me to yourself, then hold me at arm's length behind closed doors."

"I can and I will, because that's what is best for you. I'm thinking of you in this."

She snorted. "No, you're not. You're thinking of you. I knew you were a lot of things, Sol, but a coward was never one of them. You can take your protection and shove it up your ass. I don't need to be protected. What I wanted from you was so much more than that."

She stormed to the door, still wrapped in nothing but the sheet from his bed.

"Lizzie, I—"

"Save me your pity or remorse. I've had it with the people in my life acting like I'm this fragile flower that can't handle life. That should be put in a cage where nothing can touch me. I'm done with that. And I had thought, hoped, you saw me as more, but you're just like all the rest, putting me in a glass prison and acting like I'm this paragon of virtue. When you've never once asked me what I want!" The sob tore from her throat.

She wrenched open his door. Hurried to her room next door. Punched in the key code and slammed the door behind her, sliding the lock into place, with Solomon's hoarse whisper—her name—still ringing in her ears.

Chapter 13

Lizzie stumbled into the bathroom, dropped the sheet, and started the water in the bath tub. She was trembling, freezing at the glaciers that had seemingly moved into her soul. She stared at the water, willing it to fill the tub faster as her teeth chattered. She added bubble bath, and the scent of water lilies filled the air.

She climbed into the water—the temperature was just beneath scalding—to try and warm her limbs. Lizzie leaned forward to switch the water off and spied the mottled blue and purple love bite on the side of her breast. There were more over her chest. Reminders of the way his mouth had scorched a trail over her flesh.

Drops of water splashed on the back of her hand. Thick, hot tears blurred her gaze. Shutting off the water, she couldn't stop the tears from falling any more than she could stop herself from loving Solomon. And she did love him, with every fiber of her being. She always had, from the very first.

And, deep down, she knew she'd always wanted him to be her first lover. It was why she'd waited so long. She knew that now. But she'd never expected him to be the one to hurt her more than anyone else.

What a mess they'd made of things. Friendship or no, he wanted her, he did. The air sparked with desire when they were close. But she didn't understand why he thought she couldn't handle the fact that he was a Dominant. Hadn't last night proved that she could? Nor did she know how to proceed with him. All right, she had never been trained as a submissive, but she'd thought he would do the honors. That he not only would be her first love, but her last as well.

Lizzie was missing something, a key element, and she wasn't sure if that was because of her inexperience. Solomon was so controlled and had been so distant, like he'd planned on telling her to stay away from him from the moment he'd intervened the other day, kept her from being with Michael and Dante. She swiped at her tears.

Wait a minute.

Was that the key? He'd said it himself: that he never planned on sleeping with her. Which meant that, when he relaxed his control or was pushed past it, he couldn't help himself.

That didn't resolve the question as to why he felt she couldn't handle the submissive lifestyle. Lizzie could, she had enjoyed last night beyond measure, and had only wanted more of his heated, erotic touch. Sure, she had a lot to learn, and she was intelligent enough to understand not all of it would necessarily be easy. But she'd wanted to please him with a fierceness that shocked even her, yearned to sleep next to him every night, and wanted to love him until her dying breath.

She'd already do that last part, with or without him. And she would rather do it with him.

After her bath, Lizzie took her time getting ready for their first performance that day. With a seed of an idea in mind, she placed a call she half-dreaded and half-prayed would work. Then she put herself together, creating the illusion that she was unaffected by what had occurred this morning. One, because she knew Solomon. It would drive him crazy that she wasn't weeping over him. That was what he expected her to do. And while on the inside, she was—in spades—she checked her appearance in the mirror and nodded. She'd do. Two, if she was going to put her plan into action, she couldn't let Solomon read her. The man knew her too damn well and would try to stop her.

Some of it would require groveling on her part, and not to Solomon, but if the chance to get him back cost her her pride, then it was worth it. She had to try.

She tried to eat but nothing would settle. And then she was glad she'd avoided food when she walked into the lobby. The one-two sucker punch of seeing Solomon at the piano almost made her turn around and run. The only reason she didn't was because if she wanted to prove that she did belong in his world, she couldn't run and hide.

Lizzie straightened her spine and dug down deep into the farthest recesses of herself for the strength to endure. She held her head up high and waltzed over to the piano. She didn't allow her gaze to fall or show any other signs of weakness. At the music stand beside the piano, she set up her sheet music and then withdrew her flute from its case.

"Ready?" she said, proud that her voice was steady and sure.

His gaze imperceptible, he nodded. "Whenever you are."

She waited for the signal from Solomon. The first sparkling series of notes of introduction on the baby grand. Then she began, focusing on the music. She played like her heart wasn't torn in two. She played like the whole world was watching, and only showed them what she wanted them to see. It was the longest hour of her life. Moving from concerto to duet to jolly Christmas music, with every note plunging into her chest like shards of ice.

When the final note of the last song echoed in the lobby,

Lizzie packed up her flute and music. With a nod at Solomon, she said, "See you in two hours."

Then she walked away, ignoring the plaintive note in his voice when he whispered, "Lizzie."

She had an appointment in five minutes. And if she stopped, her resolve would crumble. If she was to get the help she needed to fix this, then she had to go. The elevator ride to the top floor was uneventful. Determination filled her as she strode down the hall to the office door. With a deep breath, she knocked.

"Come in."

She pushed open the door into Jared's office. He reclined behind his large desk. Michael and Dante were both already there as well. Closing the door behind her, she walked toward them on unsteady legs.

Each man, each Dom, was looking at her with a stern expression on his face. She couldn't blame them. She owed them an apology. And before they were through, she'd owe them so much more.

"Elizabeth, have a seat, and then you can explain what this meeting is all about," Jared ordered.

Ever the Dom was he. Swallowing her pride—she needed them on her side—she nodded and did what he requested. She sat in the big leather chair, feeling dwarfed by the three big, bad Doms, her stomach performing acrobatics.

"First, I need to apologize for what occurred the other day. And I need to explain why it happened. It's a little lengthy, and I hope you will listen with an open mind."

Michael tilted his golden head. "What's there to explain? You acted out against your Dom, and used Dante and me as collateral damage."

She flinched. There was a shit storm of damage control that she should have taken care of before now. She replied, "I understand how that might be how you perceived the situation but that's not accurate."

Dante snorted, and crossed his arms over his massive chest. "What tripe are you feeding us now?"

"Please let me explain and once I'm finished, if you still feel offended, I will submit fully to whatever punishment you deem acceptable at the time and place of your choosing," she promised.

"I admit, I'm intrigued. Continue," Michael said.

Lizzie explained everything, laying her cards and her deepest shame on the table. She told them about her and Solomon first meeting in college. About her strict upbringing and loveless engagement. Everything... right up to her first night on the island with Solomon and how she'd come on to him, only to be turned down.

She explained that she had gone to the club the other evening with every intention of being with another Dom. That she'd had no idea Solomon would interfere. And then she explained that, while he had relieved her of her status, something had shifted, and she had no idea what to do.

"I have no experience with any of it. But I'd like to, so that I can—"

"Win Solomon back?" Jared murmured, a hint of approval in his gaze.

"Or see if I'm crazy to even try to attempt it. If you say that it is, I will trust your judgement and leave him be. I just didn't have anyone else to go to, you see. Michael, Dante, truly I am sorry for my part in this and that you were caught up in this drama. I had every intention of being with you that night."

Dante said, "My sweet, the fact that you were going to gift Michael and me with your innocence before Solomon interfered speaks volumes."

"What do you need from us?" Michael asked, his formerly stern expression replaced with one of kindness and warmth.

"Train me to be a submissive. Without sex, if it's possible."

"It totally is, although we'd prefer it the other way. We'll make you a deal. We will train you, but if things don't work out, you'll belong to us, and spend another week here on the island as our sub, no holds barred."

As much as Lizzie didn't want another man at all, the fact that they were so willing to help her after all the shenanigans she'd put them through made her feel like she had to agree. How could she not? Besides, should her efforts fail, being with them wouldn't be a hardship. They were gorgeous alpha Doms who clearly considered a sub's needs before their own. And perhaps they'd help her pick up the shattered remains of her heart. She'd never be whole again without Solomon, but if he truly didn't want her anymore, maybe they could help her see a way to move on.

"I accept your deal. When would you like to begin, Sirs?" she asked, lowering her gaze out of respect.

Dante whistled. "I might not want to give you up after we've trained you."

"Thank you, Sir." After being tossed away like yesterday's garbage by so many men, it felt refreshing to have someone want to keep her. Even if only for a little while.

"You have two more performances today, yes?" Michael asked.

"That's correct. I have the next one in thirty minutes and then a break for two hours, then the last one is from seven to eight."

"Dante's going to escort you to your performance and then bring you to our suite once it's done. We will start your training there, with dinner. Help you dress for the evening at the club after your last performance."

She shrank back in her seat. "You want me to go to the club? But what if he causes a scene again before I'm ready? What if—"

"I will intervene on your behalf. He won't bother you," Jared interjected.

She'd almost forgotten he was there, he'd been so silent.

"You're sure?" She didn't want to start a war with Solomon. But she didn't know any other way. If, after she'd given it her all, Solomon still turned her out, well then, at least she could say she had given it everything she had.

"Yes, I am," Jared said. "Is there anything else you need from me?" he asked, glancing between Dante and Michael.

Michael scraped a hand over his pensive face. "There is, if you have another sub who is good at keeping secrets and could help us out. Since we are not going to be having sex with Elizabeth, then we will need relief, as well as someone to demonstrate some techniques."

"I have just the sub in mind. If you want to stay behind, Michael, I will call her up and we can speak with her. Elizabeth, go with Dante now, lass, to your performance."

"Yes, Sir."

Dante held out one of his big hands. Lizzie accepted it without question, hoisting her flute case and music with the other hand. As they left Jared's office, Dante said, "Let me hold those for you, my sweet."

"Thank you," she murmured, transferring them into his outstretched free hand.

They entered the elevator and Dante's dark chocolate eyes glowed with merriment. "Easy, my sweet, deep breaths. You can do this. And if you can't after this week, or Solomon ends up being a daft prick and rejects you, I cannot say I would be sorry. In fact, there's a part of me that almost hopes he does so that you will belong to us."

She smiled up at him. Dante would be easy to fall for, with his gregarious grin and devil-may-care, rakish attitude. He bolstered her flagging spirits. Going on instinct she cupped the side of his face, his stubble scraping against her palm. She leaned up on her tip toes and brushed her lips against his cheek just as the elevator stopped at another floor and opened.

It was like in one of the movie vignettes, where everything

slowed to a crawl and still frame. She lowered herself and turned. On the opposite side of the door stood Solomon, a dark, furious storm clouding his face.

"Solomon, come on board. There's room enough," Dante murmured, his arm tightening protectively around her waist.

After a brief glance between her and Dante, like he was gauging the situation, Solomon entered. When the doors had closed, Dante said, "She told us the truth: that you aren't truly her Dom, so you can stop looking daggers at us, man. She will be with us for the rest of this week."

Solomon stared at her, seeking the truth of Dante's words. Lizzie leaned into Dante, plastering a small grin on her face when really, she felt like she was dying inside. Solomon sardonically said, "Yes, well. Good luck with that."

The elevator ride from the eleventh circle of hell finally came to an end. Solomon exited first, like someone had lit his butt on fire, not sparing a glance back at her with Dante. Lizzie stared after him, trying to will him to turn around, to look at her. Was she making things worse?

"He'll come around. Just give him time," Dante murmured by her ear and then tugged her out of the elevator, leading her toward their mini stage area in the lobby. Already guests were milling about in the extra chairs and couches. Their shows were fast becoming a well-attended event.

It was strange really, she'd always turned to music as a way to soothe herself. Whenever she was down or her heart hurting, it was what she had turned to in times of crisis. But at this moment, for the first time in forever, she wanted nothing to do with music. A fact which said more about the tumultuous state of her emotions than anything else.

Dante led her through the crowd to her music stand and helped her get ready. He leaned over and whispered in her ear, "You can do this. Play to me and ignore him. Trust me on this. It's already driving him crazy, in a good way."

He laid a kiss on her forehead and she nodded. Dante took a seat in the front row, making it easy for her to concentrate on him. And then, finally, after a deep breath, she turned to Solomon. His gorgeous face was unreadable.

"Are you sure about him, Lizzie?" He nodded toward Dante.

"That's none of your concern now, is it? Shall we get this over with? Dante and Michael have a special dinner planned for me between shows."

His gaze flashed between her and Dante. If she didn't know better, she'd say he was jealous. But then, she'd never been on the receiving end of that particular emotion so she wasn't sure. The last thing she wanted to do was read an emotion that just wasn't there. Her heart was in enough agony as it was, she didn't need to add to it. But perhaps her plan might work. With that in mind, she stood her ground.

"Very well," he said in a clipped, controlled voice.

The performance was as excruciating as the first one that day had been. Technically, it worked, and the crowd gave them rapturous applause. But even to Lizzie's ears their performance fell flat. When it was all said and done, Dante was there to scoop her up and escort her back to his suite.

She felt Solomon's eyes on her back as she walked away. How had it come to this?

Chapter 14

Solomon was seething.

Un-fucking-believable!

He wanted to kill the bastard. Get a few solid punches and jabs into his pretty face. Rip his arms from his sockets for touching what belonged to him. But she didn't, did she? And why was that?

Because he was a fucking idiot.

He'd had Lizzie for the taking, could have made her his forever with a few words that he'd been too terrified to utter. Solomon had allowed the ghosts of his past to control his future. And he'd shunned her, told her he wouldn't touch her. Her face that morning, just a few short hours ago, had sliced him to the bone. And he'd put that agonized expression there. Her voice had trembled, and her broken heart had been visible in her eyes when she'd asked him if she hadn't been good.

The truth was that she had been fucking amazing. His every fantasy brought to life and then some.

He had destroyed her with his words when all he wanted to do was keep her in his bed, and had thought of nothing else but how incredible she'd felt in his arms; how right. The way her

116

body moved against his, underneath him… he could still recall her taste, and hungered for more.

But she'd taken him at his word. He'd rejected her twice now. Like a complete and utter moron.

So it shouldn't come as a surprise that she was trying to move on with someone else. The fact that it was happening right under his fucking nose did not sit well with Sol, though. As much as he knew he needed to move on, he just couldn't. She was *his* Lizzie.

How do you move on from the one person who has filled your dreams for years? When he'd told her about his decision, she'd been correct in her assumption that he was a coward, but she just didn't understand what it was he feared. Maybe if he'd explained it to her more, made her understand why, things might have been different.

And, deep down, he knew he was a fool for letting her go.

He'd loved her from the moment he met her. Solomon still remembered what she'd been wearing. The short jeans skirt with the pink sweater set. A strand of sedate pearls around her neck. Her lustrous golden hair in a high pony tail, and a gamine grin that had taken his breath away.

But she was a good girl, more suited to afternoon tea than the lifestyle. He'd known that then as surely as he knew it now. When had he become uncompromising, though? Or had he always been that way? Had his parents' actions scarred him so deeply that he'd pushed away the only good thing that had ever happened to him?

And he was a head case. Solomon didn't deserve another chance with Lizzie, regardless of whether or not he wanted one. He sucked in a breath; he needed to get some fresh air, cool his jets a bit. It was either that or he would stomp up to those block-heads' suite and go all caveman on them. Lizzie deserved better. Especially when he'd been such a heartless fool.

He strode toward the elevator but Jared appeared out of nowhere and blocked his forward progression.

"I need a word with you," Jared said, his voice low, his eyes hard and unyielding.

"Fine, I was just on my way outside for some fresh air. We can talk out there," Solomon replied, heading to the stairs instead. He didn't stop until they were on the ground level. Everyone seemed to be heading toward the hotel so he moved further afield. There was a slight bluff overlooking the marina that was blessedly empty. The scent of salt water and orchids hung heavy on the warm breeze.

Steeling himself, he turned and met Jared's steady gaze.

"I understand that you claimed Elizabeth was your sub when that wasn't the case." Jared's face didn't give Solomon a hint of what he was thinking.

"Jesus. Did she speak with a committee?" Fury and anguish swirled in Sol's chest. But if he was mad at anyone, it was himself.

"No. And here's the thing, Sol, I'm on your side in this. I think you and Elizabeth are right for one another. I've seen the way you look at her. But for some moronic reason, you seem to be pushing her into the arms of another Dom. In this case, two."

Jared had hit the nail on the freaking head.

"Yeah, so what's your point?" Dread settled in the pit of Sol's stomach.

"That you'll not interfere with her interactions with Dante and Michael."

"Why? That doesn't seem to sound like you're on my side." He snorted. What the hell was Jared playing at?

"It is from where I'm standing. You are being given a chance to see if she's what you want, or if you are going to let her go. Because, to be clear, if you let her go, she *will* find another Dom to be with. She's ripe for love and, more importantly, if you're not going to step up to the fucking plate and be the Dom she needs, she deserves someone who will."

"And you think Dante and Michael will be that for her?"

Solomon wasn't a praying man, but this instance was calling for it.

Jared slid his hands into his pockets and shrugged. "Quite possibly. I've known them for some time and I've never seen them react this way with another sub."

Solomon winced. That really was the million-dollar question, wasn't it? Was Lizzie better suited to someone else? And once she set her mind to it, was there anything she couldn't get, including a man who loved her? Had he hand-delivered her to those two on a fucking platter? He argued, "She's not a submissive though, Jared. I've known her forever. She's the Mayberry picket fence, two-point-five kids type of woman. I'll never be the vanilla type of man she needs. I enjoy the lifestyle far too much. If I gave it up for her, I would end up miserable, and that misery would cause her grief in the end. You know that, and you know you could never walk away from it either."

"Did she ask you to walk away from the lifestyle?" Jared asked with a perplexed glance.

"Well, no." *Wait, what?*

"From my point of view, I think she's very much a submissive. Untrained, to be sure, but there's an eagerness to please and a desire to learn. I think that's what makes her so appealing to Dante and Michael. An untrained sub, one willing to please, is a rare prize in our world. You know that as well as I."

Sol did. He really, truly did. And it was a knife straight through his chest. He grimaced. "Why are you telling me all of this?"

"Because you need to decide, and do it swiftly. If you truly do care about her as much as I think you do, stop being an ass and do something about it."

"But I thought you said—"

Jared tsked him, like he was a freaking submissive and missing half his brain. "You didn't let me finish. Tonight, she belongs to Dante and Michael. I'll not have my business called into question over your drama and unwillingness to choose a course of action with Elizabeth. You can't put her on a pedestal inside a gilded cage and expect her to stay where you can look at her, love her, but never touch her. That's not fair, to either of you. But especially to her. In this, you need to put her needs first."

Had Solomon done that? Put her up as this unattainable woman? Had he used the possibility of being like his father as a way to shield himself from loving her? That was an unpleasant thought. All this time, he'd worried that he was like his dad, when the truth was that his dad would never have let a woman he loved go. Solomon had. He'd pushed Lizzie away, and for what? Misplaced martyrdom?

Solomon said, "That's what I'm trying to do, man. But now that I've—never mind…" He shook his head. He knew how flimsy it all sounded, even to his ears. He'd fucked things up royally.

Jared finished for him and said, "Now that you've touched her, you can't stand the thought of her being with another? I've been where you are, but the thing is, perhaps instead of fighting what you feel for her, you could show her how good it could be between you and let her decide. She already loves you. You need to decide whether you're willing to toss it all away on the off-chance that she won't accept the lifestyle—when you never even tried it. That, my friend, is cowardice."

"Thanks for that," Sol muttered. There was that word again.

"Don't mention it. Think about what I said." Jared gave him a thoughtful stare.

"I will." Solomon vowed to stay away from the tequila, otherwise he really would go caveman on Lizzie without processing what he needed to first.

"Good. Now, if you don't need me, I'm going to go see my Naomi about dinner."

"I'll be fine. Just plan to get a little air and think over the conversation," Sol replied.

Jared gave him a salute and walked away, uttering under his breath, "Thank goodness I wasnae such a thick-headed dunce as that poor fool."

Jared had a fucking point.

Solomon turned and watched the ferries dock, the sea darkening into a deep blue cobalt as the sun began its nightly descent. Jared had certainly given him more food for thought. Had he set Lizzie on a pedestal? Turned her into this paragon? And for what? So that he could admire her from afar but never risk his heart?

Because that was what this was about. After he'd walked in on his mum with a man who wasn't his father, only to have his dad return home and end up killing the bastard, Solomon's life had been torn asunder. In some ways, he realized now, he'd never fully healed because he'd never allowed himself to. He'd used the lifestyle to blanket and cover the broken parts of him. Fuck. He wiped a hand over his face. He was a mess. How had he not seen it until now? What if Lizzie could heal him? She wasn't his mum, and it was harsh and unfair that he had somehow been putting her into the same category.

Lizzie wasn't a woman who strayed. She'd been with that rat bastard, Edward, for what, seven years? She hadn't loved him and had still never cheated on him. If there was a better woman on the planet, Sol didn't know one.

When he'd moved to America to live with his aunt, a scared sixteen-year-old with a chip on his shoulder because he'd discovered his mum hadn't been perfect, and neither had his dad, Solomon had closed himself off from deeper emotions. Instead, he'd pursued his passion for music. He'd already been gifted on the piano, but his aunt and uncle had pushed him toward Julliard and helped him get a scholarship.

Sol had always thought the world of his mum. But her carelessness and her betrayal had created a seed of distrust. He'd always thought of his mother as a paragon of virtue and later discovered she was simply a human who'd made a terrible mistake. His dad had served time for murdering her lover, eventually dying in prison, and Solomon had never forgiven his mum for the destruction she'd brought to their lives. Not until it was too late for them to have a relationship. She'd died thinking he hated her.

And perhaps, in his way, he'd wanted to protect Lizzie from the world at large. Her engagement with her ex had meant she was safe from the world—most of all, from Sol. Because he feared he was like his dad, too hot-headed and passionate for his own good, and that he'd somehow end up destroying her.

Especially with what she made him feel: so fucking much, it scared the shit out of him.

Solomon had loved Lizzie from the moment she'd waltzed into his life. But he'd held himself back, controlled his deeper feelings for her out of fear. Because the last people who'd loved him had left him to fend for himself at a young age. Christ, there was even a part of him that thought he didn't deserve love—not if he was anything like his dad.

It was one of the reasons why the lifestyle worked for him. He needed to control himself, otherwise he would turn into his father or at least, that was what he'd always feared.

But had it all been a mirage he had used to keep his heart safe? Nothing prepares you for being an orphan. And while his dad had died when Solomon was twenty, Sol didn't see him again after that fateful night when he was sixteen. His dad or his mum. He'd lost his parents when he was sixteen and had never fully recovered, because he'd not allowed himself to. He'd used his grief as a shield against any deeper interactions.

If Solomon ever hurt Lizzie the way his father had his mum, it would kill him. He feared that more than anything. So he'd kept his interactions strictly with women, with submissives, who understood the score, and ensured things never progressed beyond the physical.

But once he'd touched Lizzie, it was all over for him. And it hadn't just been this week. That one stolen kiss in Scotland, almost a year ago now, had shattered his control. A deep-seated part of him had simply declared: *mine*.

Lizzie broke through his defenses. She laid siege to his control more soundly than the *1812 Overture*. And now that he had tasted her, felt her come undone beneath his hands, his mouth, and felt the silken clasp of her pussy around his cock—Christ, he was a fool. He never should have touched her, but now that he had, he couldn't erase the hold she'd unknowingly placed over him.

His need to protect her, even from himself, had overridden all his other senses. When he'd woken up this morning with her petite body burrowed against his, all he'd wanted was to sink into her and stay. And that had rattled him to his core. He never got too close and always kept women at a safe emotional distance. It was safer for them. And Solomon was terrified at the potency of his feelings for Lizzie.

Because those feelings had always been there, since day one.

He'd seen the agony in her eyes this morning; it had mirrored his own sentiments. When she'd stormed from his room, it had taken every ounce of the strength and control he possessed not to race after her.

Could he live with himself if he let her go?

He loved her, that much was true.

He always had, and knew that when his final breath came, it would be her name upon his lips. Which made him the biggest blundering idiot on the planet. It pained him to watch her with another man, Dom or not.

At seeing her turn those big beautiful eyes up at another Dom, something inside Sol had snapped, especially since he knew now he was her first. Did he want to be her one and only? Her first and last? Or was it better if he let her go?

And would she still want him after the hell he'd put her through because of his fear?

Jared had issued blunt orders that Sol shouldn't do anything about it tonight. But should he allow a little thing like Jared's warning to stop him?

And what did he want?

The only answer that presented itself—Lizzie.

More importantly, what did he plan to do to get her back?

Chapter 15

"**O**kay, my sweet, what do you think submission is?" Dante asked. They were in the living room of his and Michael's suite. It was just as lovely as the one Lizzie had but there was an extra bedroom attached.

She sat on the couch between the two big men, feeling desolate. "It's about giving up control."

"It's more than that," Michael murmured.

"The truth is much of the power within a Dominant and submissive relationship lies with the submissive. She or he makes the conscious choice and puts themselves in the care of the Dom," Dante said.

"And it's not all about the sex either, although that part doesn't hurt," Michael added with a sexy grin.

"I'm not sure I understand your meaning, Sirs."

"Think about it like this: you are entrusting your body, your heart, and your mind to a Dom. In turn, it is the Dom's responsibility to ensure that his submissive is properly cared for on all levels. A good Dom will see to his submissive's needs before his own."

"That sounds nice," she admitted. It was what she craved,

since no one had ever made sure she was taken care of, not even her parents. But still she worried her bottom lip. Would Solomon even come near her if he thought she'd slept with Michael and Dante? That was the one little hiccup she didn't see a way around.

"You have a desire to please others, that's evident in the way you handle yourself," Michael said.

"And you are a passionate creature as well. I've seen you play. We both have. You don't just play the notes, you make love to them. Watching you play is a sensual, erotic experience. I know I've been rock hard by the end of your performances," Dante admitted, letting her see the hunger in his glance.

"Well, I'm not sure about that," she replied.

"Why do you doubt your worth? You're a gorgeous creature and managed to turn our heads, but you don't seem to believe you are desirable. Why is that?" Michael asked.

She fidgeted under their gazes. She really didn't want to talk about this. It was her biggest shame.

When she would have ignored the question, Dante placed his forefinger beneath her chin and turned her face toward him. "One of the biggest components about being a submissive is that you must be honest with your Dom in all things. It appears to us that you haven't had that many opportunities to open up to anyone. You wanted our instruction, wanted to use us as your test subjects, so use us. Show us the parts that you think are broken— without fear of reprisal. Part of a Dom's mission is to help his sub move past her hurts. We can't do that unless we know what they are."

She grimaced. "But doesn't it make a submissive sound whiny or ungrateful? I've had a ton of advantages, and it makes me feel like a spoiled brat to admit I didn't get everything I wanted growing up."

"And what was it you wanted?" Michael asked.

"For my parents to love me. I mean, in their way, I know they lid. But they never showed it. Even as a child, if I skinned my knee and wanted a hug, I got a lecture on what not to do so that there wouldn't be a skinned knee in the first place."

At that, Dante hefted her onto his lap, his big arms cradling her. She tensed, wondering what he was going to do. They'd agreed: no sex.

"Relax, my sweet, this is about giving you some of that affection you missed out on. Don't think, just enjoy. Take a few deep breaths and let yourself relax into me," Dante commanded.

She did as he asked, letting his heat and warmth sink into her. She was shocked when the tears started. How long had she been holding that inside? Only her whole life. She'd craved hugs and kisses, had wanted to curl up in bed with her mom after a nightmare, only to be treated like she was untouchable. She'd had to contain or put aside her natural exuberance and flair just so her parents would accept her. Lizzie's childhood had been one big empty sea of loneliness, never understanding why it was wrong for her to yearn to just be hugged. So she'd sunk all of those feelings and needs into her music.

It was safe there; the sounds, the perfect pitches, the way the notes blended from one haunting, gorgeous sound to another were what she'd held close and where she'd let her passion and exuberance for life reside. In some ways, she supposed she should thank her parents for their distance. Without it, she probably wouldn't have practiced so hard and worked like a dervish chasing excellence. But her achievements had also been the only time they'd ever shown her praise.

She nearly jumped out of her skin at the second touch of hands, caressing and kneading her back muscles.

"Easy, just relax," Michael commanded softly.

It wasn't easy. Lizzie was typically a ball of tension. But as the Dom duo soothed her, she felt peace wash over her. Then she realized that no matter what, she would survive. Perhaps not well, and if Solomon shut the door on her completely there was a part of her that would die along with it, but there was companionship and comfort. It may not be burning with passion and tearing up the sheets. It may not be love.

It wouldn't be exactly what she wanted, but she would survive.

At the knock on the door, she started in Dante's arms.

"I'll get it," Michael said, leaving them on the couch. "Thanks for coming, Miriam. We appreciate your willingness to help us out."

"Certainly, Sir. I'm here in whatever capacity you need me," Miriam said. Her red curls swayed as she took in the room, her gaze absorbing Lizzie, still cuddled on Dante's lap.

Michael shoved the door closed and then placed a hand on Miriam's lower back and led her over to the seating area. Dante shifted Lizzie in his lap so that she was facing both Miriam and Michael.

"Miriam, please strip for me and get into submissive pose," Michael ordered.

Miriam did as he asked, removing her work uniform, folding the clothes, and placing them on the nearby coffee table before she knelt down. Her thighs were slightly spread, her feet flat. She placed her hands on her knees and bowed her head.

"Very nice," Michael murmured, caressing Miriam's head almost as if he was petting her. But Miriam's pleasure was not lost on Lizzie. Miriam's body softened beneath his touch and praise. Then Michael's gaze lifted to Lizzie. "Now it's your turn, Lizzie. I want you on your knees and trying this pose."

"Yes, Sir," she murmured.

Dante shifted her off his lap and she whimpered at the loss of his heat. Dante was like a big, raging furnace, keeping her warm.

"Strip first," Michael ordered.

"What?" Her gaze shot between Dante and Michael's unyielding expressions.

"That's what, *Sirs*, my sweet," Dante said.

"I don't understand, Sirs. I thought we agreed on no sex." She was too raw emotionally to be able to share her body with another man.

Michael gave her a calm stare, and said, "This isn't about sex. This is about submitting your will to us. About pleasing us."

"I'm sorry, and I don't mean to question you, but I don't understand what my being naked has to do with training me and teaching me to be submissive… Sirs," she said.

Dante interjected, "It's about learning to follow a Dom's command, even when you don't quite understand the why of it. In a true Dom and sub relationship, for it to work, a sub must be willing to act without question. It's about placing your full trust in that Dom to provide for you."

Miriam murmured quietly and asked Michael, "May I speak, Sir?"

Michael gave her a gentle smile and said, "Yes, you may."

Miriam turned her soft emerald gaze Lizzie's way and said, "I submit because it takes all the worries and cares I have away. I find peace there, knowing I will be taken care of without question, and trusting that the Dom has my best interests at heart."

Michael gave her an approving smile, then bent down and gave Miriam a heated kiss as a reward. It was unique for Lizzie to watch how fluid Miriam's body was as she leaned into the kiss. She didn't hold herself back or chicken out.

Dante murmured, standing near her, "What's it to be, my sweet? We can't help you, train you, if you're unwilling to follow the simplest of directives. I get that you're afraid and that people who were supposed to be there for you failed you, time and again. But in this, you will have to take the leap, be brave, and trust us. Or we're done. Not because of spite, but because we can't train someone who's unwilling to bend."

Lizzie was afraid. Dante was right. How had she not seen it? And she'd thought she was this confident, independent woman, when the reality was that she walked around with an invisible shield about herself, never allowing herself to get attached to anyone out of fear that they wouldn't love her or show her affection of any kind. And that was the thing with Solomon. He'd pushed past her defenses, knocked her barriers down, and heaped hugs and pure joy upon her. Was it any wonder she loved him? Or that she'd been so afraid to tell him how she felt about him—because she feared losing the one person who'd always cared for her and shown it, and not just paid her lip service.

And the thing was, she wanted to give Solomon what he needed. The man had been her anchor, and the only one keeping her from becoming a bitter old maid. In more ways than one. Without further judgement or recourse, she did as they asked until she was standing before the two Doms in her birthday suit.

"You're lovely, my sweet. Now, into submissive pose, please," Dante ordered.

Lizzie slid to her knees, double-checking Miriam's pose as she arranged her body into position.

"Good, again," Michael said.

"You're going to practice until you are able to do it fluidly," Dante advised.

This went on for a good fifteen minutes until they had her stop. Then they practiced standing submissive pose, again, until they were satisfied she could assume the position without hesitation.

"Now, I would like you to kneel in submissive pose and watch as I have Miriam suck my cock. Since you are new to lovemaking in general, I want you to watch how she performs," Michael said.

Lizzie gulped and nodded. Then she whispered, "Yes, Sir."

She did as he requested, kneeling down as she'd been taught.

Michael's broad erect shaft emerged from the confines of his pants and he held his turgid member out for Miriam, like he was offering her a treat. Lizzie guessed that, in a way, he was. Then Dante leaned behind her, his breath fanning over her nape, and said, "We want you ready for tonight. We plan to do a scene with you at the club. Nothing sexual, but we want to make sure you can control your body, as well as show you how to suck a man's cock."

Miriam apparently had no qualms about her audience. Her lips were already open, her tongue swiping against the crown of Michael's impressive manhood before she sucked him into her mouth. It was hypnotic, watching the display. And, if Lizzie were honest with herself, it was rather hot too.

Lizzie felt her nipples harden and her breasts swell. Her breathing became shallow and her face flushed as she stared, transfixed. And through it all, she imagined doing that with Solomon for an audience because he asked her to. Moisture trickled down her inner thighs. Her sex pulsed. It was one of the most erotic displays she'd ever witnessed.

Especially once Michael took over. His hands held Miriam's head as he pumped his shaft into her mouth. She hollowed her cheeks and Michael gritted his teeth, then trumpeted his pleasure as he spurted inside her mouth. Miriam's throat worked, moving as she swallowed his cum.

"Something tells me you liked watching, hmmm?" Dante said near Lizzie's ear.

"Yes," she admitted, without shame.

Dinner was delivered shortly thereafter. Michael and Dante spent the next hour feeding Lizzie and Miriam. Dante had Lizzie sit near his feet on a cushion, and fed her juicy tidbits of meat, vegetables, cheese, and fruit. She understood it was about learning to concede her control over to a Dom. And perhaps she should have been appalled, but she wasn't. While she understood how some might construe it negatively, she was enthralled.

When it was nearly time for Lizzie's last performance of the day, Michael unearthed a jewel-toned, turquoise teddy for her to wear. The silk bust covered her cleavage while giving them a nice push up. There was guipure black lace detail over the center that led up to a black collar. There were removable garters that she attached sheer black stockings to. And there was also a snap crotch, for easy access for the enterprising Dom. Her ensemble was completed with a pair of black 'fuck me' pump stilettos.

Miriam helped Lizzie with her hair, fashioning it into an intricate French braid with wisps of gold framing her face. Then she applied smoky eyeshadow and liner to make Lizzie's eyes appear luminous.

"Well now, aren't you a picture, my sweet? Miriam, you've been wonderful. Thank you," Dante said, wrapping Lizzie's arm around his forearm.

"Miriam, if you could stay here, we will be back at, say, ten. I have a feeling Dante and I will have need of you," Michael commanded.

Miriam bowed her head, a smile hovering on her lips, and she replied, "Yes, Sir. I'm honored that you would ask."

"Good. Go take a bubble bath and prepare yourself for our return," Michael ordered.

He didn't have to tell her twice. She moved at hyper speed into the bathroom.

"Ready for this?" Michael asked as they escorted her to the elevator.

"As I'll ever be," Lizzie responded.

Chapter 16

Lizzie entered the lobby, flanked by Michael and Dante. Solomon wasn't at the piano yet, which was odd. The man was always on time, and could be downright anally retentive when it came to performances. But she worried that maybe she'd pushed him too far by forcing Michael and Dante in between them, regardless that her intentions were good. After all these years, she'd never known him to miss a concert. Her legs wobbled a bit at the thought.

Oh, god, what if she had miscalculated?

As much as she told herself she'd survive, the thought of living without him was unbearable. Pain lanced through her body and stole her breath. She delved deep into herself and found the strength to carry on as if nothing untoward had occurred. It wasn't easy, though.

With trembling hands, Lizzie arranged her sheet music on the stand, then withdrew her flute from its case, making sure it was ready for the performance. She turned toward Michael and Dante, with every intention of keeping her gaze fixed on them as they talked. But then the elevator doors opened, and Solomon entered looking like sex on a damn stick.

Bare chested, he strode in wearing nothing but black leather pants, riding low on his hips, and shit-kicker boots. He was dark and dangerous. And every single part of her being registered his presence. His eyes caressed her frame with a look that caused her knees to quake. It was raw and elemental, and reminded her of how he'd looked when he had been buried inside her the last time.

Her heart thumped in her chest. She didn't understand. What new torture had he devised?

Solomon had told her that he wasn't the man for her, with no room for argument and with finality. Now he was dangling himself before her like a freaking carrot. Had he not done enough damage already? Her heart was raw, bleeding, and broken at his feet. Her flute shook in her hands. And she cursed the fact that Solomon was the only one who had ever made her lose her composure in front of an audience.

Dante, bless the man, rescued her when he noticed her distress—thankfully before she did something inherently stupid, like throw herself at Solomon's feet and beg him to take her back. Dante pulled her into a hug and whispered, "Relax, deep breaths. I don't know what his game is, but we'll help you. Focus on us during the show."

She nodded against his chest, blinked back her tears, and inhaled deeply. But his scent was all wrong. It wasn't the woodsy, spicy scent she adored. That was because he wasn't Solomon.

"Lizzie. Problem?" Solomon asked from the piano the moment Dante stepped away and reclaimed his seat.

She turned and glanced at him, keeping her face impassive. "No. Why do you ask?"

"If you're not up for doing the show—"

"It's fine. Let's get this over with, please," she said, unable to keep the exhaustion from her voice. All they'd done was go back and forth with one another. As much as she wanted to live with passion, she didn't want the heartache and pain that were accompanying it. Maybe she really was built incorrectly, which was why Solomon just didn't want her for more than a few nights. It was a depressing thought, but perhaps closer to reality than she'd like to admit.

With a deep breath, she lifted her flute into position. The weight of her instrument felt familiar in her hands, the smooth surface a comfort that steadied her. She waited for the first notes from Solomon. As their resonance glided on the air, she slid into the performance. Her heart was in this one. Her heartache trilled and tempered every sound. This was where her world made sense. She understood the rules, the tempo, the time signatures, the key signatures. Nothing else mattered for Lizzie in this moment than each song, every cadenza, and melody, which she wrapped around herself like a protective, warm blanket.

When she finally lowered her flute, she realized there was wetness coating her cheeks. Lizzie didn't say anything as she gathered her belongings. She was unable to look at Solomon, because then he would see how utterly pathetic she was, and if she ever wanted to right her world, she couldn't.

"Lizzie, can we talk?" Solomon asked quietly. The low timbre skittered along her spine. The simple request nearly brought her to her knees—and would have, if it weren't for the two Doms watching her back.

Michael and Dante flanked her, with Dante placing a steadying palm against her. Not looking over her shoulder, she shook her head and muttered, "I can't, Sol."

Then Michael and Dante ushered her away from the alcove and the man who'd held her heart forever, it seemed. The Masters of Underworld protected her as if she were their own, and gave her the fortitude to walk away. She couldn't stop the tremors as they headed toward the elevator banks.

A series of chords rang out in the lobby and brought her to a standstill. He wouldn't, would he?

When Solomon's deep baritone joined the melody, she shuddered. Why? Why would he do this?

"Come on, my sweet, keep moving," Dante whispered. Dante and Michael tried to lead her to the elevators but she refused them. Withdrew from between them as she turned and stood rooted to the spot, batting their hands away.

It was their song. Hers and Solomon's. Whenever they had been goofing off at Julliard during practice, or when he'd played with her in the symphony, they would end up performing the song together. She could remember that first time, after a particularly brutal rehearsal at Julliard. Sol had invited her over to his bench and begun the tune. By the end, they were laughing like drunken loons and singing loudly off-key, but it had forged their bond with one other, deepened it, and become an unspoken promise between them that they would always be there for one another.

She couldn't hear Billy Joel's *Piano Man* without thinking of him. Lizzie could be on the other side of the globe performing, hear that song, and would text him. *La, da, de-de, da-a.* And he'd reply with the other half.

Her heart thumped madly beneath her breast.

The naked emotions upon Solomon's face were clear as he beheld her, and she stared, transfixed. He was singing, playing, for her. Lizzie felt every note and bar, every word as his beautiful voice sang for her, to her. It was the soundtrack of their friendship. The folks milling in the lobby had stopped to listen, the entire atmosphere a frozen tableau. She felt Michael and Dante standing near her back, still guarding her. None of it mattered.

Then Solomon finished. The last note hung in the air like crystal resonance, his gaze never wavering from her as he stood. He advanced, erasing the distance between them, and approached her. The lobby, normally bustling with activity and voices, was so silent, she could hear her own harsh breathing.

Solomon, her big, beautiful, stubborn man and best friend, came to a standstill a mere foot from her. And she sensed Michael and Dante take a step back and retreat, so that it was just the two of them—with their audience.

Solomon's gunmetal stare caressed her, and then his voice, infused with husky emotion, said, "Lizzie, I'm so sorry. I never meant to hurt you, and know that I have done my fair share this week. I've been letting my fear of becoming like my father rule my emotions and the decisions I've made for my life. It doesn't excuse my treatment of you. If you'll give me a chance to explain so I can make things right—"

Some of the wind deflated from her sails. Lizzie murmured, "I already know about your parents. Do you think I don't know you and all your secrets after thirteen years?"

Surprised flitted across his face, then shifted into acceptance. His hands at his hips, he shook his head, obviously chagrined, and said, "No, I didn't realize it. I'm not sure how you know."

"Your aunt told me years ago, when I asked," she admitted. There was little she didn't know about the man, from the way he liked his coffee, to the shampoo and cologne he preferred. She'd been with him to help celebrate his graduation from Julliard, and again when he'd gotten a contract to play for the London Symphony Orchestra, through everything, right up to him recording his own music.

He flashed a small, mindful grin. "Priscilla's always been fond of you. But I used that fear to keep myself from getting too close, and kept myself from loving you."

Lizzie's heart dropped into her toes. She whispered, too afraid to hope, "What are you saying?"

Warmth and profound emotions permeated his gaze and every part of her being responded in kind. He said tenderly, "Mia bella, I love you. I have been in love with you since you stumbled into my practice hall, all pink and golden. I'm so sorry that's it's taken me thirteen years to figure that out. I was wrong, the biggest moron imaginable, to turn you out and say that we didn't belong together, because we do. There's no one else for me because it's always been you, Lizzie. And if you'll let me, I will make it up to you. I swear to do right by you."

"How?" she asked, her fists clenched at her sides. Hope beat a rhythm in her heart. Her gaze never vacillated from his.

"Marry me. Be my wife, my partner, and the love of my life. Now. Tonight. Be mine in every way, and I will spend the rest of our lives showing you how much I love you. Derek is willing and standing by in his captain's capacity to do the honors down on his boat as we speak."

She wondered if it was all a dream and then Solomon said, the smile that reminded her of the day they first met spread across his lips, "What do you say, Lizzie? Love me, forever?"

Joy erupted in her heart. And then it was her turn to show him what he meant to her. No longer afraid, Lizzie shocked him and slid to her knees, arranging herself into the submissive pose she'd learned that day. With her heart and soul in her eyes, she lifted her teary gaze to his. Then she said, "Whatever my Sir wants."

The lobby broke into boisterous applause. And Solomon, love shrouding his features, hauled her up into his arms and kissed her, claiming her for everyone to see. She wrapped her arms around his neck, pouring herself and the love she held for him into her kiss.

Solomon broke away first. His hands cupped her face, his eyes searched hers, seeking reassurance. He asked, "You're sure?"

Joy burst in a cacophony as she touched him, running her hands over his back with unabashed pleasure. He was hers and she was never letting him go. "Yes. I love you, Solomon. There's no one for me but you. You were my first, and I want you to be my last, my only. I've never wanted anyone except you."

The sexy smile he gave her filled her heart. He nipped her bottom lip and said, "Then let's go make it official and legally binding in every way."

She couldn't agree more and said, "I thought you'd never ask."

Chapter 17

Lizzie married Solomon a short time later aboard *The Leg Spreader* in her turquoise teddy, with Solomon wearing his leather pants. Jared acted in her father's stead and gave her into Solomon's keeping. On board the vessel, Michael and Dante stood in attendance after telling her to be happy, along with as many people who could fit on the boat without sinking it. Including Miriam, whom Dante had retrieved from their shared room so that she didn't miss the fun and festivities.

The news about the impromptu nuptials had spread quickly over the island. Residents and guests alike lined the docks to witness the joyful event.

With the moonlight shining down upon them, Lizzie promised Solomon to love, honor, and cherish him. The love in Solomon's eyes awed and humbled her as she spoke her vows. And she couldn't stop her blissful tears from falling as he said his vows. Solomon surprised her at the exchanging of the rings, producing a small platinum band with a single solitaire diamond that he slipped over her finger, and a dark titanium band for himself. The man had thought of everything.

When Derek proclaimed them husband and wife for all to

hear, a great cheer erupted along the beachfront docks. Solomon's eyes—the naked emotion in them as he kissed her as her husband for the first time—made the rest of the world fall away. He would always be her everything. When he finally released her lips, he twined his hand through hers as they were congratulated by everyone.

They accepted handshakes and felicitations as they left the boat, with Jared promising to throw them an impromptu reception the following day. Her hand clasped in Sol's, her heart happier than it had ever been, Lizzie let him lead her away from the crush of people and up to their room. They'd move her things in in the morning. Lizzie didn't plan on either of them wearing clothing for the rest of the night if she could help it.

Inside their room, they discovered a special dinner that had been delivered while they were at the docks. It was full of finger foods, meat and cheeses, oysters, fruit, a crusty French loaf—all meant with lovers in mind. Beside the loaded tray on the dining table was a champagne bucket with two bottles of chilled Cristal and a pair of crystal flutes.

And then Solomon twirled her into his arms and gave her an unrepentant, wicked gaze. "So, Mrs. Ventura, what would you like first on our wedding night? Are you hungry? It looks like the chef went all out for us."

Lizzie glanced up at him, amazed at the love she saw there. They were married. Solomon, her best friend—the man she'd loved her whole life, it seemed—was now her husband. She slid her arms up his bare chest, thrilled that she could touch him, hold him, love him whenever she wanted. She said, "I just want you, Sol. Take me to bed and love me. The rest can wait."

"With pleasure," he murmured, and hoisted her into his arms. He carried her over to the bed, where he proceeded to show her, in exacting detail, just how much he loved her. When he finally slid inside, he cupped her face, his gaze boring holes into hers with such fierce love, she trembled.

"No regrets?" he asked.

She traced her hands down his back, overjoyed at the turn of events and ecstatic at the way he felt beneath her fingertips. She said truthfully, "None. You?"

"Only that it took me so long to figure out how much you mean to me. But now that you're mine, I am never letting you go. I love you, Lizzie. Forever won't be long enough."

"No, it won't be, but it's certainly a place to start. I'm game if you are."

"Forever, then, mia bella."

"Yes, my love, forever," Lizzie replied.

Solomon covered her mouth, his lips brushing over hers in a kiss filled with the promise of all the sweet tomorrows. No longer was Lizzie untouched or unloved, but had finally found where she belonged.

She knew that no matter how long she lived, or how much they loved, forever wasn't long enough for her duet with her piano man.

~THE END~

Anya Summers

Born in St. Louis, Missouri, Anya grew up listening to Cardinals baseball and reading anything she could get her hands on. She remembers her mother saying if only she would read the right type of books instead binging her way through the romance aisles at the bookstore, she'd have been a doctor. While Anya never did get that doctorate, she graduated cum laude from the University of Missouri-St. Louis with an M.A. in History.

Anya is a bestselling and award-winning author published in multiple fiction genres. She also writes urban fantasy and paranormal romance under the name <u>Maggie Mae Gallagher</u>. A total geek at her core, when she is not writing, she adores attending the latest comic con or spending time with her family. She currently lives in the Midwest with her two furry felines.

Don't miss these exciting titles by Anya Summers and Blushing Books!

The Dungeon Fantasy Club Collection
The complete set of all eight full-length, scintillating, spicy romance novels!
Her Highland Master
To Master and Defend
Two Doms for Kara
His Driven Domme
Her Country Master
Love Me, Master Me
Submit to Me

Her Wired Dom

Visit her on social media here:
http://www.facebook.com/AnyaSummersAuthor
Twitter: @AnyaBSummers
Goodreads: https://www.goodreads.com/author/show/
15183606.Anya_Summers
Sign-up for Anya Summers Newsletter

Connect with Anya Summers:
www.anyasummers.com

Blushing Books

Blushing Books is one of the oldest eBook publishers on the web. We've been running websites that publish spanking and BDSM related romance and erotica since 1999, and we have been selling eBooks since 2003. We hope you'll check out our hundreds of offerings at http://www.blushingbooks.com.

Blushing Books Newsletter

Please subscribe to the Blushing Books newsletter
to receive updates & special promotional offers.

You can also join by using your mobile phone:
Just text BLUSHING to 22828.